Nina Moore Tiffany

Pilgrims and Puritans

the story of the planting of Plymouth and Boston

Nina Moore Tiffany

Pilgrims and Puritans
the story of the planting of Plymouth and Boston

ISBN/EAN: 9783337287177

Printed in Europe, USA, Canada, Australia, Japan

Cover: Foto ©Andreas Hilbeck / pixelio.de

More available books at **www.hansebooks.com**

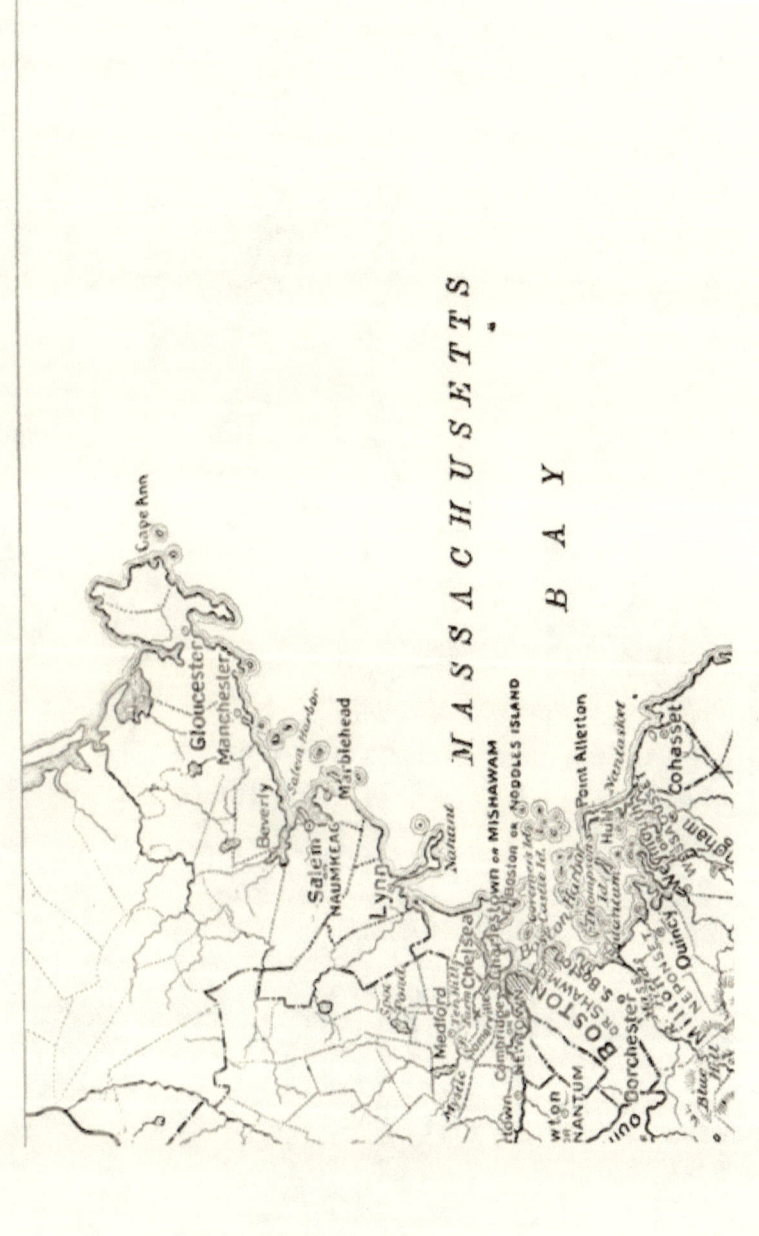

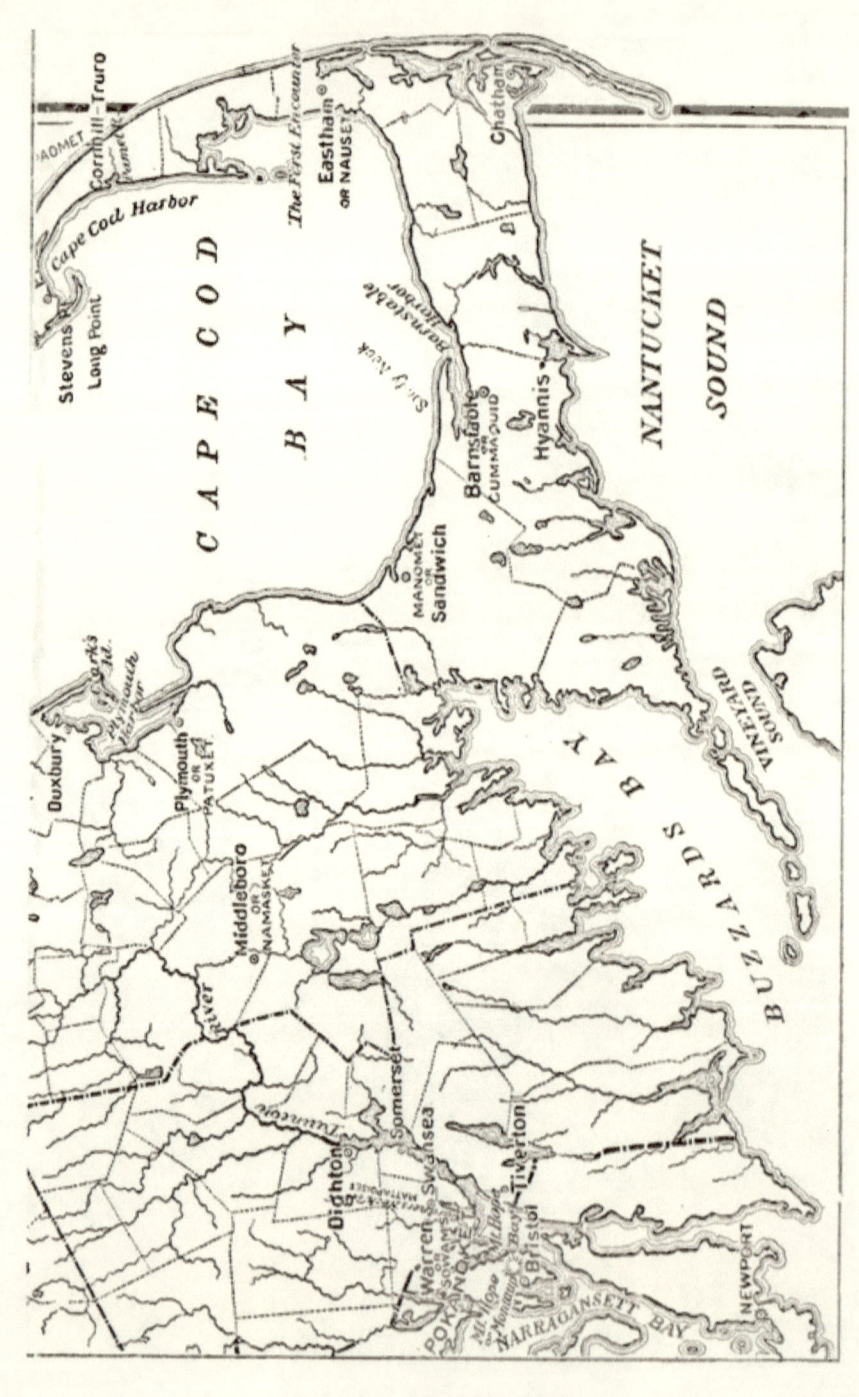

PILGRIMS AND PURITANS:

THE

STORY OF THE PLANTING OF PLYMOUTH AND BOSTON.

BY

N. MOORE.

GINN & COMPANY

BOSTON · NEW YORK · CHICAGO · LONDON

The Athenæum Press

GINN & COMPANY · PRO-
PRIETORS · BOSTON · U.S.A.

PREFACE.

THE story of the settlement of Plymouth, told by Bradford and Winslow, and that of Boston, found in Winthrop's Journal, have the unfailing charm of personal narrative and the value accorded to all first sources of history. To present the substance of these stories in a setting which shall bring them within the comprehension of young readers, and with such maps and notes as may prove useful in the schoolroom, is the purpose of this little volume.

NINA MOORE.

CONTENTS.

MAPS AND ILLUSTRATIONS.

SEPARATISTS AND PURITANS IN ENGLAND.

I.

JAMES AND THE SEPARATISTS.

WHEN James I. became king of England, he tried, as English kings and queens had tried before him, to enforce obedience to one sovereign church. " I will have," he said, "one doctrine, one discipline, one religion in substance and ceremony."

The wishes of his people mattered little to him, — " I will govern," ran his haughty speech, " according to the common weal, but not according to the common will."

To protest was vain, — " It is . . .," said he, " high contempt in a subject to dispute what a king can do, or to say that a king cannot do this or that."

He believed firmly that "a king is above law by his absolute power," and that "a king can do no wrong."

Hoping to maintain absolute power he allied himself with the bishops of the English Church; and insisted that the same church service and the same church ceremonies should be performed in every English parish.

In many of the parishes there were men who disapproved of parts of the service and of many of the ceremonies. They wished to worship God in a way purified from certain old-time customs, and were therefore called, mockingly at first, Puritans. The Puritans refused to conform to the church. James said that they must conform.

"I will make them conform," said he, "or I will harry them out of this land, or worse."

Then some of the Puritans, believing that they had a right to judge for themselves in such matters, broke away from the church and formed separate congregations of their own. One of these congregations met at Scrooby.

CHARLES I.

As James's threats were followed by persecution, the Scrooby Separatists fled to Holland. There, outcasts from their country and wanderers for the sake of their religion, they began to speak of themselves as Pilgrims. In time they crossed to America and settled at Plymouth.

II.

CHARLES AND THE PURITANS.

The Puritans who remained within the church clung to it, hoping for better days; but James died, and Charles came to the throne, and still their trials did not cease.

Charles had learned well his father's maxims, "a king can do no wrong," "a king is above law"; and soon proceeded to practise them.

An English sovereign is bound, in law, to have a body of men, a parliament, to help him rule. Charles ruled alone, without a parliament, for many years. By his folly he lost all hold upon the people, and when the Scots rose in rebellion against him, for trying to make them accept some of the ceremonies of his church, his English subjects joined them in a civil war.

The war ended in a defeat for Charles. He was dethroned, and at last beheaded.

After this the Puritan Independents had matters all their own way for a time; but the change came too late to benefit those whom Charles's rigor had driven from their homes. During his lifetime, before the war broke out, a large number of Puritans had left England to begin at Salem and Boston the Colony of Massachusetts Bay.

THE POKANOKET AND MASSACHUSETTS INDIANS.

THE country settled by the Pilgrims and Puritans was overrun by savage hordes of straight-haired, copper-colored men to whom Columbus had given the name of Indians.

War was their main business, but the New England Indians, though far from peaceful, had been somewhat tamed by planting cornfields and building villages.

Their villages could be built in a day and removed in an hour, for these people, wandering from their cornfields to their hunting-grounds and thence to the river-weirs as the seasons changed, made for themselves no real homes; their dwellings were but places of shelter from cold and rain. A traveller writes: " I have seen half a hundred of their wigwams together in a piece of ground, and they show prettily; within a day or two, or a week, they have been all dispersed." Yet some of their rude hamlets stood for years.

"Their houses, or wigwams, are built with small poles fixed in the ground, bent and fastened together with barks of trees, oval or arbor-wise on the top. The best sort of their houses are covered very neatly, tight and warm, with barks of trees slipped from their bodies at such seasons when the sap is up; and made into great flakes with pressures of weighty timber, when they are green; and so becoming dry, they will retain a form suitable for the use they prepare them for. The meaner sort of wigwams are covered with mats they make of a kind of bulrush. . . .

"These houses they make of several sizes . . . some twenty, some forty feet long and broad. Some I have seen of sixty or a hundred feet long and thirty feet broad. In the smaller sort they make a fire in the centre of the house; and have a lower hole on the top of the house, to let out the smoke.

"They keep the door into the wigwams always shut, by a mat falling thereon, as people go in and out. This they do to prevent air coming in, which will cause much smoke in every windy weather.

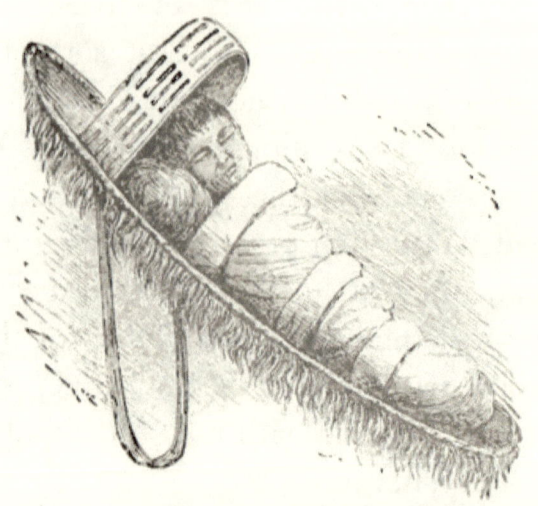

AN INDIAN CRADLE.

"If the smoke beat down at the lower hole, they hang a little mat, in the way of a screen, on the top of the house, which they can with a cord turn to the windward side, which prevents the smoke. In the greater houses they make two, three, or four fires. . . . I have often lodged in their wigwams; and have found them as warm as the best English houses.

"In their wigwams they make a kind of couch of mattresses, firm and strong, raised about a foot high from the earth; first covered with boards that they split out of trees, and upon the boards they spread mats . . . and sometimes bear-skins and deer-skins. These are large enough for three or four persons to lodge upon; and one may draw nearer or keep at a more distance from the heat of the fire, as they please, for their mattresses are six or eight feet broad.

"Their food is generally boiled maize, or Indian corn, mixed with kidney-beans, or sometimes without. Also, they frequently boil in this pottage, fish and flesh of all sorts, either new taken or dried. . . .

"Also they mix with the said pottage several sorts of roots; as Jerusalem artichokes and ground-nuts and other roots, and pompions and squashes and also several sorts of nuts or masts, as oak-acorns, chestnuts, walnuts. These, husked and dried and powdered, they thicken their pottage therewith.

" Also sometimes they beat their maize into meal and sift it through a basket made for that purpose.

" With this meal they make bread, baking it in the ashes, covering the dough with leaves. Sometimes they make of their meal a small sort of cakes, and boil them.

" They make also a certain sort of meal of parched maize. This meal they call nokake. It is so sweet, toothsome, and hearty that an Indian will travel many days with no other food but this meal, which he eateth as he needs, and after it drinketh water. And for this end, when they travel a journey or go a hunting, they carry this nokake in a basket or bag, for their use.

" Their household stuff is but little and mean. The pots they seethe their food in . . . are made of clay or earth, almost in the form of an egg, the top taken off. . . .

" Their dishes and spoons and ladles are made
of wood. . . . Their pails to fetch their water in
are made of birch barks, . . . doubled up, that it
hath four corners and a handle in the midst. . . .
From the tree where the bark grows they make
several sorts of baskets, great and small. . . .
Some of their baskets are made of rushes, some
of bents, others of maize husks, others of a kind
of silk grass, others of a kind of wild hemp, and
some of barks of trees. . . .

" The baskets and mats are always made by
their women; their dishes, pots and spoons are
the manufacture of the men.

" . . .The Indians' clothing in former times
was . . . skins of beasts, as deer, moose, beaver,
otters, raccoons, foxes and other wild creatures.
Also some had mantles of the feathers of
birds. . . .

" Their ornaments are, especially the women's,
bracelets, necklaces, and head-bands of several
sorts of beads, especially of black and white
wampom. . . .

" The wampompague is made . . . of a part

of the wilk's shell. The black is of double value to the white. . . . With this wampompague they pay tribute, redeem captives, . . . in a word, it answers all occasions with them as gold and silver doth with us.

". . . Their weapons . . . were bows and arrows, clubs and tomahawks made of wood like a pole axe, with a sharpened stone fastened therein; and for defence they had targets made of barks of trees.

". . . For their . . . travels, and fishing, they make boats, or canoes, . . . of great trees, pine or chestnut, made hollow . . . which they do by burning them, and after with tools, scraping, smoothing, shaping them.

". . . They make another sort of canoes of birchen bark, which they close together, sewing them with a kind of bark, and then smearing the places with turpentine of the pine-tree.

". . . They used to . . . oil their skins and hair with bear's grease . . . and then paint their faces with vermilion or other red, and powder their heads.

" Also they use black and white paints, and make one part of their face of one colour and another of another, very deformedly. The women especially do this, and some men also, especially when they are marching to their wars and hereby, as they think, are more terrible to their enemies. . . . The men, in their wars, do use turkey or eagle's feathers stuck in their hair. . . .

" They are much given to hospitality in their way. If any strangers come to their houses they will give him the best lodging and diet they have. . . .

" There are among them certain men and women whom they call powwows. . . . These are sent for by the sick and wounded."

The powwows used a strange mode of cure. " The manner of their action . . . is thus : The parties that are sick are brought before them; the powwow sitting down, the rest of the Indians give attentive audience, . . . and after . . . many a hideous bellowing and groaning he makes a stop, and then all the auditors with one voice utter a short canto. Which done, the powwow still proceeds in his invocations, sometimes roaring like a bear, other times groaning like a dying horse, foaming at the mouth like a chafed boar, smiting on his naked breast and thighs with . . . violence. . . . Thus will he continue sometimes half a day."

The Indians herded in small tribes or clans, each having its petty chieftain; while the clans were grouped in larger tribes under a general sachem. Thus the Massachusetts Indians, inhabiting the country between the hills of Milton and the coast, formed one group of allied clans; the Pokanokets, living further toward the south, another. These two groups were closely connected, at times even coming under one government.

The Massachusetts sachem once held dominion over the Neponset, Nonantum, Punkapoag, and many other clans, and could call about him a large force of warriors. Squantum Farms, in old days called the Massachusetts Fields, was the gathering-place of the tribe. There the war councils were held, and there, too, were the cornfields and fishing-weirs.

Massasoit, the sachem of the Pokanoket group, lived sometimes at Montaup, now Mount Hope, sometimes at Warren, which in his day was Sowams.

The Pokanokets included the Patuxets or Plymouth clan; the Nausets, who were at East-ham; the Namaskets of Middleborough; the Pocassets of Swansea, Rehoboth, Somerset, and Tiverton; the Mattachees of Cummaquid, or Barnstable; and other tribes, besides the Wam-panoags, Massasoit's especial men.

The Pocassets were led by Corbitant, who would have liked to reign in Massasoit's stead; the Mattachees, by Iyanough, from whom Hyannis was named; and the Nausets, by As-pinet. Of the Patuxets little is known. In 1614, when Captain John Smith visited Cape Cod, their village stood at Plymouth; in 1619 the village and the clan had disappeared.

Smith had barely escaped with life from other Indians along the coast, but the Pokano-

kets received him well. He, in turn, gave them
fair treatment; and was much displeased when
Hunt, the master of his second vessel, repaid
their kindness with treachery.

This Hunt, lingering at Cape Cod after
Smith had gone, seized a number of the Patuxet Indians, seven of the Nausets, and three
from Cummaquid, and sailed with them for
Spain.

" He betrayed four-and-twenty of these poor
savages aboard his ship," wrote Captain Smith,
indignantly, "and most dishonestly and inhu-
manly for their kind usage of me and all our
men, carried them to Maligo, and there, for a
little private gain, sold these silly savages for
rials of eight."

Among the Patuxets thus stolen was an Indian named Squanto, or Tisquantum. Squanto
was not left in Spain, but was taken to London, where he lived for a while with a Mr.
John Slanie, in Cornhill. Mr. Slanie afterward sent him to Newfoundland, where he was
found by another Englishman named Dermer.

Captain Dermer, who was about to explore the New England coast, took Squanto into his service as a guide, and in 1619 sailed with him for Cape Cod.

On arriving with Dermer at Patuxet, Squanto found his old home desolate, his friends "all dead." No living person was in sight, to wonder at or to rejoice over his return.

Pushing on further into the country, the two travellers learned that a great plague, which was only then abating, had attacked the Indians, killing them by scores. Men scarcely healed told them of its ravages. Among the Wampanoags but sixty warriors remained, and of Tisquantum's people none, not even a woman or a child.

The Massachusetts tribe, also, had nearly vanished. Obbatinewat, sometimes called the sachem of Shawmut,[1] still led a wretched life in his old haunts, wandering from place to place for fear of the " Squaw-sachem" and of the Tarratines; a chief named Chickataubot, with a

[1] Now Boston.

handful of followers, took Neponset for his abiding-place; Pecksuot and Wituwamat, two petty chieftains, dwelt somewhere in the forest; but the power of the Massachusetts group, like that of the Pokanokets, was gone; and the English, coming not long afterward, easily took possession of the shore.

THE PILGRIMS.

I.

THE FLIGHT FROM ENGLAND.

EARLY in the reign of James the First, a certain William Brewster lived in what remained of the old manor house, at Scrooby. He was a staunch Puritan, Non-conformist, and Separatist, and had gathered a congregation of Separatists about him.[1] Each Sunday saw people from the surrounding villages wending their way toward his house to listen to the sermons of Mr. Clifton, their teacher, or of their pastor, Mr. Robinson.

One of the most active members of the congregation was William Bradford, whose home was in the neighboring hamlet, Austerfield.

---

[1] They were called Non-conformists because they would not conform to the established church; Separatists, because they had separated from it.

SITE OF THE MANOR HOUSE AT SCROOBY.

The large tree is said to stand on the site of the main building ; the manor house itself has long since gone.

Bradford had been left, as a child, in the care of his uncles. They believed firmly in the king's church; but he, when only seventeen, withdrew from that church, and joined the Scrooby Separatists.

The king was determined to force the Separatists to conform, and punished severely those who refused to do so.

"Some were taken and clapt up in prison, others had their houses beset and watched night and day, . . . and ye most were fain to flie and leave their houses . . . and the means of their livelihood."

But even to fly was difficult. James had said that he would "harry them out of the land, or worse"; and now, when the Pilgrims tried to leave England for Holland, he showed them what that "worse" might be. His officers were told to seize all who attempted to go.

"There was a large company of them purposed to get passage at Boston in Lincolnshire, and for that end had hired a ship wholly to themselves, and made agreement with the

master to be ready at a certain day, and take
them and their goods in.... So after long
waiting and large expenses, though he kept
not day with them, yet he came at length and
tooke them in, in ye night. But when he had
them and their goods aboard, he betrayed
them, having beforehand complotted with y^e
searchers and other officers so to doe; who
tooke them and put them into open boats
and there rifled and ransacked them, search-
ing them to their shirts for money."

These "catchpole officers" stripped them not
only of their money, but also of their books
and other goods, and having done that, took
the whole company back to the town, where
they were imprisoned, some for a month, some
for a longer time.

On becoming free again, Bradford and his
friends formed yet another plan.

They found a Dutch captain who promised
to take them on board his vessel at a point
between Grimsby and Hull, far from any town.

The women and children, with the goods,

NORTH

SEA

were sent to this place in a small bark, and, arriving first, put into a shallow creek to wait. Unluckily, the ship came at low tide, when the bark lay stranded on the mud, and its passengers could not be taken off.

The men, meanwhile, were walking impatiently about on shore, and one of the boats of the ship set out to fetch them. The first boat-load had hardly been taken on board the vessel when a body of armed pursuers was seen hastening across the fields; and the Dutchman, alarmed for his own safety, "swore his country's oath (sacrament), and having the wind fair, weighed his anchor, hoisted sails, and away."

The men thus carried off were nearly in despair at leaving their families and possessions at the mercy of the officers; but though the women and the children were detained in England for a time, they were finally allowed to go, and, with the rest of the Pilgrim Church, at last joined their friends in Holland.

II.

THE VOYAGE TO AMERICA.

For the next eleven or twelve years the Pilgrims tried to make an English home in Holland for their children and their church.[1]   But

they could not keep to English customs in a foreign land, nor could they hope to spread

[1] Home of the Pilgrims in Leyden, as seen in 1670.   " No. 1 is the bell-turret (no longer standing) of the cathedral which stood at 2, and beneath which Robinson was buried.   No. 10 is the house in which Robinson lived, with a garden on the hither side, the front being at the other end of the building. on the Klog-steeg or Clock-alley, marked 5."   [*Narrative and Critical Hist. of America, Winsor.*]

their sombre religion among the pleasure-loving Dutch. Instead of this, they saw their young people fast turning into worthy mynheers and vreows, and their church suffering more here from the Sunday pastimes of the people than it had ever suffered in England from the wrath of James.

Poverty, too, distressed them, and they were alarmed by threats of a coming war. For all these reasons they decided to make still another change, — to begin an English colony in America.

A tract of land near Hudson River was granted them; and though the king would make them no promises, he allowed their messengers to understand that their church was not likely to be molested in his new realm.

The younger and stronger members of the congregation then made ready for the journey. They were to go first, to break the way. Among them were John Carver, William Bradford, William Brewster, and Edward Winslow; and they had been joined by a soldier, Myles

Standish,[1] who was to become the most famous of them all.

Two vessels had been engaged to carry them across the ocean, — the Speedwell, lying at Delftshaven; and the Mayflower, which was taking on supplies at Southampton, England.

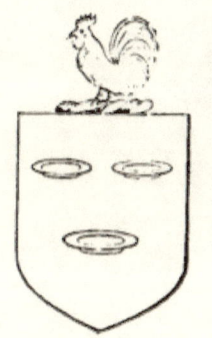

After a sad parting at Delftshaven, the Speedwell joined the Mayflower, and set sail with her along the English shore.

Very soon, however, the Speedwell sprung a leak, and they put in at Dartmouth for repairs.

Repairs proved of no avail; she had gone but a short distance farther when her captain declared her to be unseaworthy, and they turned back, this time entering the port of Plymouth, on the southern coast.

Here the Pilgrims sifted their company anew. About twenty people withdrew to leave space for the rest, while those who were best

[1] STANDISH COAT-OF-ARMS. *Arms:* Az. three standishes arg. *Crest:* A cock arg. *Motto:* Constant en tout.

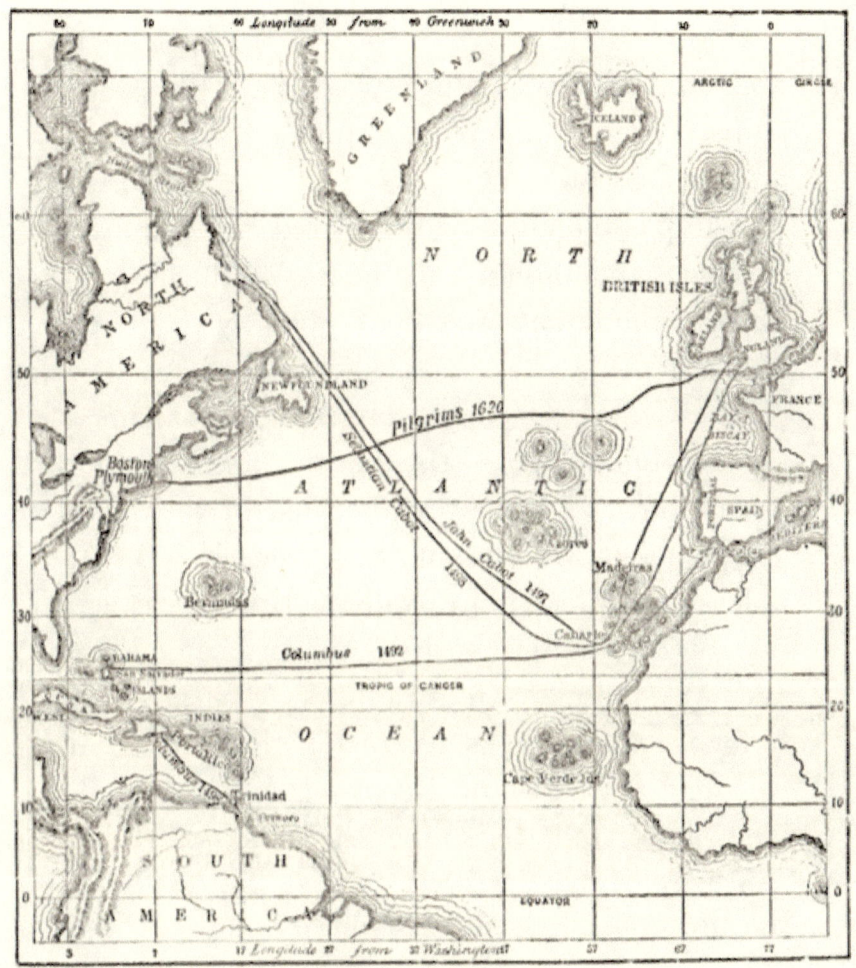

VOYAGES OF DISCOVERY.

able and wholly willing to endure the hardships before them, crowded into the Mayflower and pushed on.

The passengers now numbered one hundred and two, and though one man died during the voyage, the count was kept good by the birth of a child.

This child, Oceanus Hopkins, was named for his birthplace, — the ocean; and another, born later, was Peregrine, because of the peregrinations of his parents and himself. But it is less easy to say why William Brewster called one of his daughters Fear, or his sons Love and Wrestling. In Bradford's writings the latter is spoken of as "Wrastle" Brewster, and we read there also of Resolved White, Humility Cooper, and Remember Allerton.

When about half-way across the Atlantic the little vessel was racked by storms, and one of the beams of the mid-ships bowed and cracked. For a time the Pilgrims thought they must turn back, but a great screw brought the beam into place again, and the Mayflower was held to her course.

" After long beating at sea they fell in with that land which is called Cape Cod." This was not the region they were seeking, so they " tacked aboute and resolved to stand for ye southward . . . to finde some place aboute Hudson's river. . . . But after they had sailed y^t course aboute half ye day they fell amongst dangerous shoals and roaring breakers."

Because of these shoals and breakers and " ye wind shrinking upon them withal, they resolved to bear up againe for the Cape, and thought themselves happy to gett out of those dangers before night overtook them, as, by God's providence, they did. And ye next day they gott into ye Cape harbor, where they ridd in safety."

III.

DISCOVERIES.

THEY now gave up all thoughts of going further, and decided to settle near this quiet bay.

A shallop which had been stowed away in

the ship's hold was therefore taken out, and the carpenter set to work upon it, to fit it for a voyage of discovery in the shallow water of the coast and inlets.

But Standish would not wait for the repairing of the boat. With Bradford and fourteen others he went ashore at Stevens's Point, hoping to find and treat with the natives, or at least to explore the hills and streams.

"When they had ordered themselves in the order of a single file and marched about the space of a mile, by the sea, they espyed five or sixe people, with a dogge, coming towards them, who were savages, who, when they saw them, ran into the wood and whistled the dog after them."

Standish and his men pursued, but could not overtake them; so, as night was coming on, they stopped where they were, kindled a fire, set three sentinels, and rested on the ground till morning.

By dawn they were up and away, following in the track of the Indians.

DESCRIPTION OF THE MAP.

At *a*, near what is supposed to have been a pond, the women were set ashore to wash clothes.

At *b*, Standish saw the Indians and dog.

At *c*, *d*, the Indians disappeared into the woods, and ran up the hill.

At *e*, the first night was spent.

Near E. Harbor Village they drank their first N. E. water.

At *g*, they built a fire as a signal to the ship.

At *h*, North Truro, they spent their second night.

At *k*, they opened a grave.

At *l*, Cornhill, they dug up some corn.

After reaching Pamet River they turned back.

At *i*, near E. Harbor Village, Bradford was caught in a deer-trap.

At *t*, near Great Pond, the third expedition passed their first night.

At *y*, near Great Meadow Creek, the third expedition passed their second night and had the first encounter with the Indians.

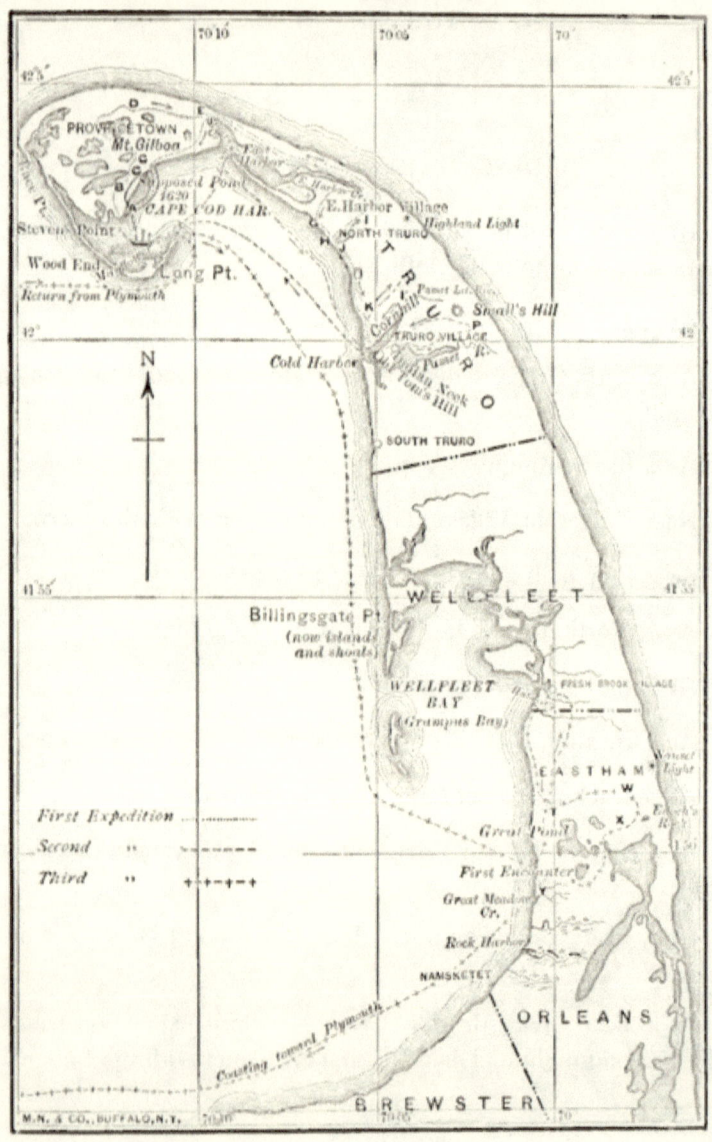

" Thorow boughs and bushes and under hills" they marched, tearing even their armor, growing more hungry and thirsty every hour, but finding no houses or people.

At last they came to a valley of fresh springs where they saw a deer. " We were heartily glad," they write, "and sat us downe and drunke our first New-England water with as much delight as ever we drunke drinke in all our lives."

Next they saw some heaps of sand, and from one of the heaps dug a buried bow and some arrows. These mounds, they thought, were Indian graves, so they "put the bow in againe, and made it up as it was and left the rest untouched," thinking that it would be "odious" to the savages to have strangers "ransack their sepulchres."

Walking on through a field or two of stubble, they arrived at another mound, — not a grave, this time, but a granary, — where they dug up "a fine great new basket, full of very fair corn ... with some six and thirty goodly ears of corn; some yellow, and some red, and others mixed with blue, which was a very goodly sight."

As they were in need of the corn, they took it with them, trusting that they might afterward find and pay the owners.

Wandering through the woods, on their way back to the ship, they came upon an Indian deer-trap, — "a young sprit, bowed down over a bow, and some acorns strewed underneath." The manner of its working was shown in a way that caused them some amusement, for while they stood looking at it, "William Bradford, being in the rear, when he came up looked also upon it, and, as he went about, it gave a sudden jerk up, and he was immediately caught by the leg."

After freeing him they continued on their way; marching "some while in the woods, some while on the lands, and other while in the water up to the knees"; till at length they came near the ship, shot off their pieces as a signal, and were taken on board the vessel.

As soon as the shallop was ready, a second set of explorers was sent out. These men found more corn and also saw two empty Indian dwellings.

"The houses were made with long young sapling trees bended and both ends stuck into the ground; they were made round, like unto an arbor, and covered downe to the ground with thicke and well wrought matts, and the doore was not over a yard high, made of a matt to open; the chimney was a wide open hole in the top, for which they had a matt to cover it close when they pleased; one might stand and goe upright in them; in the midst of them were foure little trunches knockt into the ground, and small stickes laid over, on which they hung their pots and what they had to seethe; round about the fire they lay on matts, which are their beds."

In the houses were "wooden bowls, trays and dishes, earthen pots, hand-baskets made of crab-shells wrought together, also an English pail."

Outside were "sundry bundles of flags and sedge, bulrushes and other stuff to make mats."

This party returned to the ship without having seen any very good place for building, and November passed while various plans were being discussed.

One important act marks the month: the Pilgrims made a formal compact with each other, in which they called themselves a "body politic," with power to make laws and enforce obedience. At the same time John Carver was declared their governor.

IV.

THE FIRST ENCOUNTER.

On Wednesday, the sixth of December, Standish, Carver, Bradford, Winslow, and others set out for a third search, — their last.

By this time winter had begun in earnest. "The weather was very cold, and it froze so hard, as the spray of the sea lighting on their coats, they were as if they had been glazed."

Toward evening they landed, made a barricade of logs and boughs, and, setting one of their number to watch, betook themselves to rest.

"When morning was come, they divided their company, some to coast alonge ye shore in ye boate, and the rest marched through ye woods to see ye land, if any fit place might be for their dwelling.

"So they ranged up and doune all y^t day, but found no people, nor any place they liked." That night, as they lay about their fire within their three-sided shelter, "they heard a hideous and great cry, and their sentinel called, 'Arme, arme'; so they bestirred themselves and stood to their armes and shot off a couple of muskets, and then the noise ceased."

They thought it only a pack of wolves, and threw themselves upon the ground again to finish their sleep. But in the early gray of the morning, when they had risen and were about to eat, they again "heard a great and strange cry," sounding like "wo-ath, wo-ach, ha ha hach wo-ach!" and uttered by the same voices that they had heard in the night.

They were not long in doubt; "one of their company . . . came running in and cried 'Men! Indians, Indians!'"

The "great and strange cry" was, indeed, an Indian war-whoop; the Nausets, whose arrows now began to fly thick and fast about the barricade, were come to avenge the injury done to their tribe years before by Hunt.[1]

"Captain Myles Standish, having a snaphance[2] ready, made a shot, and after him another." Then more shots were heard from the shallop, for some of the party were defending that; then came a pause for reloading and a shout from the boat for "a firebrand, to light their matches." At this one of the party snatched a log from the camp fire, shouldered it, and marched with it through the shower of arrows to the men in the boat, while the rest

---

[1] The master of one of Smith's vessels. He carried off a number of Indians and sold them as slaves. [See p. 17.]

[2] A snaphance is a musket with a flint lock.

"called unto them to know how it was with them," and caught the answers, "Well!" "Well!" from every one, followed by the hearty cry, "Be of good courage."

The firing had kept the Indians at a distance, yet "there was a lusty man, and no less valiant, stood behind a tree within half a musket shot, and let his arrows fly at them. He was seen to shoot three arrows. He stood three shot of a musket, which were all avoided, till one taking full aim at him, . . . made ye barke or splinters of ye tree fly about his ears, after which he gave an extraordinary shriek, and away they wente, all of them."

Hastening to ask if any of the party were wounded, Standish found that not one of them was "either hurte or hitt, though their arrows came close by them and on every side of them, and sundry of their coats, which were hunge up in ye barricade, were shot through and through. Afterwards they gave God solemn thanks and praise for their deliverance, and gathered up a bundle of their arrows, and

sente them into England . . . by yᵉ master of yᵉ
ship, and called that place yᵉ first encounter."

Setting off from "The First Encounter,"
they sailed in search of a harbor. In the
course of the afternoon a storm came on;
"they broke their mast in three pieces, and
their sail fell overboard in a very grown sea,
so as they had like to have been cast away,
yet by God's mercy they recovered themselves,
and having yᵉ flood with them, struck into yᵉ
harbore. . . . And though it was very dark and
rained sore, yet in yᵉ end they gott under yᵉ lee
of a smalle island and remained there all yᵗ
night in saftie." [1]

The next day they dried their drenched
clothing and rested on the island; "and this
being the last day of yᵉ week [Saturday,
Dec. 9], they prepared there to keep yᵉ Sabbath. On Monday [Dec. 11], they sounded
yᵉ harbor and founde it fitt for shipping; and
marched into yᵉ land, and found divers corn

---

[1] Clark's Island, named so for Clark, the master's mate, who
was with them, and was the first to step upon its shore.

EW Y

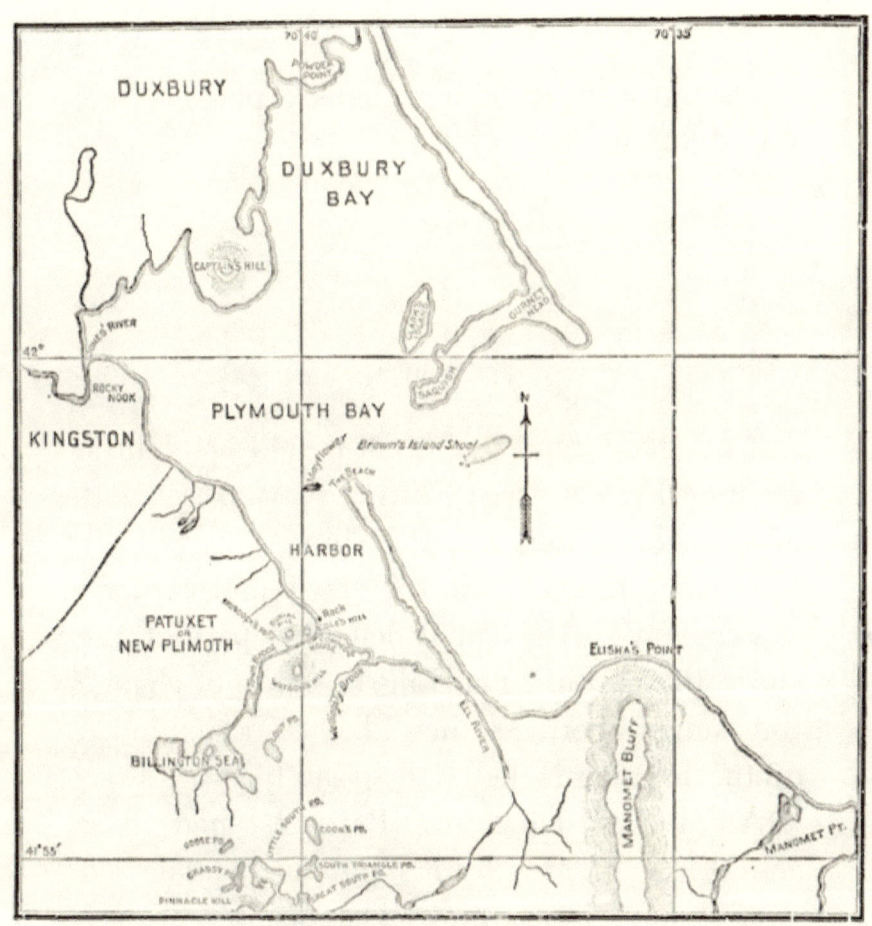

PAUTUXET, OR PLYMOUTH

fields and little running brooks, a place ... fitt for situation."[1]

V.

PLYMOUTH.

THE good report of "corn fields and little running brooks" pleased the weary passengers of the Mayflower, and the ship, safely piloted, soon came to anchor in the new-found harbor.

Prince Charles had called this part of the shore Plymouth. The Pilgrims did not change the name. Perhaps they liked to be reminded of the Plymouth they had so lately left.

An Indian tribe, the Patuxets, had lived among the Plymouth hills, but the plague had swept the tribe away. The stubble in the fields was now several years old, the brook-

[1] The anniversary of that marching into the land is our " Fore-father's Day." As the Pilgrims reckoned time the date was the 11th of December, but the anniversary of what was for them the 11th is for us the 21st.

sides were deserted. No one disputed with the
English their right to claim the soil.

A site for their town was chosen, and on
Christmas Day the first house was begun.

Their Christmas record runs: "Monday, the
25th day, we went on shore," that is, the men
of the company did so; "some to rive and
some to carry, so no man rested all that day."

And no child was the merrier for that first
Christmas time in the new world. Christmas
was a church holy-day which the Pilgrims
would not keep. The services, the carols, the
games, and the gifts with which the English
Christmas had been marked were here all set
aside. The mother could not have slipped
so much as a ring or rattle into the stocking,
— even if the child had worn one — of Oceanus
or of Peregrine. I think those Puritan babies
would have stiffened in their cradles at the
sight! Their fathers, at least, were proud to
chronicle that "no man rested" all that day.

Had they been more fond of rest, the work
which lay before them could not have been

done. Had they been less earnest in their grim religion, their strength would have been unequal to the task. Upborne by love of God and of the life which they believed he had commanded them to lead, they hewed down trees, dragged heavy logs, and endured pain and hunger as though each homely act were but another form of praise.

By their joint labor the first rude hut, a storehouse for their goods, was quickly finished. Then, every man who had a wife and children on the Mayflower began to build for them and for himself a like small cabin of rough logs; with a filling of mud mortar, windows of oiled paper, and thatched roof.

Unmarried men, or those whose wives had not yet come, were taken into one or another of these households, and the company was thus reduced to nineteen families. Nineteen house-plots were laid out, but by the time seven dwellings had been raised there was no need of more. Anxiety, exposure, and fatigue, as well as the long stay on shipboard, brought mortal illness among the Pilgrims; during that first winter half of their number perished.

William Bradford writes: " Mr. Edward Winslow his wife dyed the first winter. . . . Captain Standish his wife dyed in the first sickness.[1] . . . Mr. Molines, his wife, his sone and his servant dyed. . . . Only his daughter, Priscilla, survived."

Bradford himself was very ill. " Being at work," he was "vehemently taken with a griefe and a paine. . . . It was doubted that he would have instantly died, . . . but he grew a little better towards night, and in time, through God's mercy in the use of means, recovered."

The soldier, Standish, now turned nurse. At one time he and six others, among them Brewster and Carver, were the only men well enough to take charge of the sick. Bradford says gratefully that these friends "spared no pains night or day, but . . . fetched them woode, made them fires, dressed them meat, made their

---

[1] Her name was Rose.

beds, washed their loathesome clothes, cloathed and uncloathed them; in a word did all ye homely and necessary offices for them . . . without any grudging in ye least."

Their loss was terrible. "There died sometimes two or three of a day; . . . of one hundred and odd persons scarce fifty remained."

But read what Mr. Robinson, their old minister, wrote them from Holland: "In a battle," he said, "it is not looked for but that divers should die. It is thought well for a side if it get the victory, though with the loss of divers if not too many or too great. God, I hope, hath given you the victory after many difficulties."

Victory, then, seemed far away, for while the sick lay helpless in their beds, Indians were lurking near the settlement, watching stealthily the movements of the strangers.

To hide from the savages the weakness of the little colony the graves of the dead were levelled and the burial-place was turned into a field of grain.

VI.

SAMOSET, SQUANTO, AND MASSASOIT.

THE Indians proved shy of approach. They made signs of defiance from the top of Watson's Hill, and seized upon some tools left in the woods, but vanished if pursued.

The settlers were astonished, therefore, when one day a dusky figure strode down their village street, crying aloud, " Welcome, Englishmen ! "

" He very boldly came all alone and along the houses straight to the rendezvous, where we intercepted him, not suffering him to go in, as undoubtedly he would out of his boldness. He saluted us in English and bade us welcome, for he had learned some broken English among the Englishmen that came to fish at Monhiggon [Monhegan]." This was Samoset, an Indian from Maine.

Samoset stayed over night and went away on Saturday morning, only to come back again on Sunday with "five other tall proper men; they had every man a deer's skin on him and the principal of them had a wild cat's skin, or such like, on the one arm. . . .   They are of complexion like our English gipsies: no hair, or very little on their faces; on their heads long hair to their shoulders, only cut before; some trussed up before with a feather, broad-wise, like a fan; another a fox-tail, hanging out. . . . They sang and danced, after their manner, like antics.   They brought with them in a thing like a bow case, which the principal of them had about his waist, a little of their corn pounded to a powder, which, put to a little water, they eat.   He had a little tobacco in a bag; but none of them drank but when he liked.[1]   Some of them had their faces painted black, from the forehead to the chin, four or five fingers broad, others after other fashions, as they liked. . . .   They brought us all our tools again, which were taken in the woods. . . .

[1] We do not find these writers saying "smoke." "To drink tobacco" is their phrase.

Because of the day [Sunday] we dismissed them so soon as we could."

The next time Samoset appeared in Plymouth he brought with him Squanto, who came as a forerunner of the great sachem, Massasoit.

Squanto was a native of Plymouth, or Patuxet, though he had long since ceased to treat that as his home. He had been stolen from his country by the English, and during his long absence had learned to speak the language of his captors and to value English comforts and English power. He came to claim for his chieftain the friendship of the settlers, and to announce that Massasoit was at hand.

Indeed, in an hour's time, Massasoit, with his brother Quadequina, and a band of sixty warriors stood in full view on Watson's Hill. At first they would not venture down into the valley, nor were the settlers in any haste to cross the brook; but Squanto went back and forth with friendly messages, until both sides gained greater confidence.

EDWARD WINSLOW.

Then Winslow, with knives, a copper chain, and food as presents for the savages, mounted the hill and remained as a hostage with the Indians; while Massasoit in his turn marched down with twenty of his followers and was escorted by Myles Standish to the place of interview, — a half-finished house, hurriedly made splendid with "a greene rugge and three or four cushions."

To this house came the governor, "with drumme and trumpet after him and some few musketeers."

Massasoit, it is said, "marvelled much" at the trumpet, and some of his men "would sound it as well as they could," which probably was not well at all.

The sachem was "a very lusty man . . . grave of countenance and spare of speech; in his attire little or nothing differing from the rest of his followers, only in a great chain of white bone beads about his neck; and at it, behind his neck . . . a little bag of tobacco which he drank and gave us to drink.

"His face was painted with a sad red, like murrey, and oiled, both head and face, that he looked greasily."

No courtesy was withheld, however, — "after salutations, our governor kissing his hand, the king kissed him, and so they sat downe."

They then "treated of peace, which was that neither he nor his should do hurt" to any of the Plymouth people; in return for which the Plymouth people promised to protect him against his enemies, assuring him that King James "would esteem him his ally"; and the visit ended in content for all.

VII.

ADVENTURES OF THE FIRST SUMMER.

In April the Mayflower went back to England. Hard though the winter had been, not one of the Pilgrims returned with her. Indeed, John Alden, who had come with permission to go or stay, now freely chose to abide with the rest.

"He stayed," said Bradford, "and married here."[1]

After the departure of the ship, "as many as were able began to plant their corn, in which service Squanto stood them in great stead, shewing them both yᵉ manner how to set it, and after how to dress and tend it."

Squanto had come to live among the Plymouth settlers. He acted as interpreter between them and his people and aided the Pilgrims in many ways.

The deaths among the colonists were fewer as the spring advanced, but "whilst they were busy about their seed, their governor [Carver] came out of yᵉ field very sick, it being a hott day; he complained greatly of his head and lay downe and within a few hours his senses failed, so as he never spake more till he dyed, which was within a few days after."

Bradford was given Carver's place as governor.

In June or July, "having in some sorte or-

---

[1] He married Priscilla Mullins.

dered their business at home, it was thought
meete to send some abroad to see their new
friend, Massasoit." Edward Winslow and Ste-
ven Hopkins were charged with the undertaking.

Carrying a "horseman's coat of red cotton,
laced with a slight lace," a suit of clothes, a
chain and smaller presents, and guided by Tisquantum, they set out for Pokanoket, Massasoit's home.

It was a two days' journey. The party
spent the first night in the open fields beside
an Indian weir upon the Taunton River. The
next day they passed through tracts of well-
cleared land, unplanted since the plague, and
coming to a ford, began to cross; whereat two
old men, Indians, the sole survivors of their
clan, "ran very swiftly and low in the grass"
on the opposite bank to challenge them.

They, "with shrill voices and great courage,
standing charged upon us with their bows,"
says Mr. Winslow, "demanded what we were,
supposing us to be enemies. . . . But seeing
we were friends, they welcomed us with such

food as they had; and we bestowed a small bracelet of beads on them."

Massasoit was away when Winslow arrived at Sowams, but was sent for, and soon returned to receive his guests.

" Massasoit being come, we discharged our pieces," Mr. Winslow writes, "and saluted him; who, after their manner, kindly welcomed us, and took us into his house and set us down by him, where, having delivered our . . . message and presents, and having put the coat on his back and the chain about his neck, he was not a little proud to behold himself; and his men also to see their king so bravely attired."

" For answer to our message, he told us we were welcome; and he would gladly continue that peace and friendship which was between him and us; and for his men, they should no more pester us as they had done; also that he would send to Paomet;[1] and would help us with corn for seed according to our request."

---

[1] To find the owners of the granaries at Cornhill, that the Pilgrims might pay for the corn taken thence.

" . . . He lighted tobacco for us and fell to dis-coursing of England and of the king's maj-esty. . ."

" Late it grew, but victuals he offered none, for indeed he had not any. . . . So we desired to go to rest. He laid us on the bed with him-self and his wife, they at the one end and we at the other, it being only planks laid a foot from the ground, and a thin mat upon them. Two more of his chief men, for want of room, pressed by and upon us; so that we were worse weary of our lodging than of our journey."

" The next day being Thursday, many of their Sachems, or petty governors, came to see us. . . . About one o'clock Massasoit brought two fishes that he had shot. . . . These being boiled, there were at least forty looked for a share in them. The most ate of them. This meal, only, we had in two nights and a day. . . ."

" . . . On Friday morning, before sun-rising, we took our leave and departed, Massasoit being both grieved and ashamed that he could no bet-ter entertain us. . . ."

To feast in time of plenty, to fast when food was scarce, was always the Indian's way. A stocked larder and appointed hours for eating were quite unknown even in the household of a chief.

John Billington, a mischievous boy, who once had nearly set fire to the Mayflower, was the cause of a second expedition among the Indians.

He strayed away from the settlement, and the governor, upon making inquiries for him, learned through Massasoit that he was in the hands of the Nauset tribe.

It seems he had lost himself in the woods; and after wandering for five days with nothing to eat but roots and berries, reached Manomet and was carried thence to Nauset.

The Nauset Indians had already, at "The First Encounter," shown that they were hostile to the English; a white man could venture among them only at the risk of his life; but the boy must not be left unrescued, and ten men were sent in search of him.

Sailing first to Barnstable harbor, they spent the night at Cummaquid.

"One thing was very grievous unto us at this place," runs their account. "There was an old woman, whom we judged to be no less than a hundred years old, which came to see us because she never saw English, yet could not behold us without breaking forth into great passion, weeping and crying excessively. We, demanding the reason of it, they told us she had three sons, who, when Master Hunt was in these parts, went aboard his ship to trade with him, and he carried them captives into Spain (for Tisquantum at that time was carried away also), by which means she was deprived of the comfort of her children in her old age. We told them we were sorry that any Englishman should give them that offence, that Hunt was a bad man, and that all the English that heard of it condemned him for the same; but for us, we would not offer them any such injury, though it would gain us all the skins in the country. So we gave her some small trifles, which somewhat appeased her."

The sachem of Cummaquid, pleased with his visitors, went on with them to Nauset, where he landed with Squanto to find Aspinet, and demand the boy.

The tide ebbed while the shallop waited near the shore, and as she lay aground, the Nausets crowded about her. Here the owner of the unpaid-for corn made himself known, and was assured that if he would visit Plymouth he should have full compensation for his loss.

"After sunset Aspinet came with a great traine, and brought the boy with him, one bearing him through the water; hee had not less than a hundred with him, the halfe whereof came to the shallop side unarmed with him, the other stood aloofe with their bows and arrowes. There he delivered us the boy, behung with beades, and made peace with us, wee bestowing a knife on him, and likewise on another that first entertained the boy and brought him thither. So they departed from us."

Well content with the result of their journey, the party returned homeward, — a report that Massasoit was in danger adding to their haste.

On reaching Plymouth they found that Mas·
sasoit was indeed threatened by one of his chieftains, Corbitant, who was at Namasket, trying
to stir up a revolt.

To Namasket, then, went Squanto, to see
what Corbitant was about.

Now Corbitant hated Squanto, for making
peace between the white men and the Indians.

" If Squanto were only dead," said Corbitant,
"the English would have lost their tongue."

So Corbitant beset Squanto's wigwam and
took him prisoner; but Hobamok, another
interpreter, who was with Squanto, ran, breath-
less, back to Plymouth, for aid from Captain
Standish.

Standish marched promptly to Namasket.
At dark he stationed his nine men around the
house where Corbitant was supposed to be, and
boldly entering the low door, demanded the
chief.

The frightened savages scattered at sound of
his voice; three, trying to escape from the hut,

were wounded by the guard outside. Corbitant himself, however, was nowhere to be seen.

Hobamok, learning this, sprang to the top of the hut and called loudly for Squanto and Tokamahamon. They came, followed by a troop of trembling natives. These were assured that the white men "would not at all hurt their women or children"; whereat several half-grown boys clamored loudly, "Ne-en squaes!" "I am a woman!"

Food and tobacco were timidly brought to the invaders; then Standish, with utter fearlessness, ensconced himself in the chief's wigwam for the night.

In the morning, after leaving word that vengeance should fall upon Corbitant and all his tribe if Massasoit or any friends of the English were troubled further, the little band marched back to Plymouth, taking with them two of the wounded Indians, whose hurts were tended at the settlement and speedily cured.

"After this they had . . . much firmer peace; yea, . . . this Corbitant himselfe used ye mediation of Massassoyte to make his peace, but was shie to come neare them a longe while after."

In September Captain Standish visited Massachusetts Bay.   He noted the many islands of what is now Boston Harbor, landed perhaps at Thompson's Island, and also at Squantum, explored part of the Mystic River, and returned to the Plymouth settlers, wishing that they "had been seated there."

VIII.

FEASTING AND FAMINE.

Twenty acres of Indian corn and six of pease and barley had been planted in the spring of 1621.   In the autumn the settlers gathered their first harvest.

The pease were come to nought; but the barley, wheat, and corn had yielded fairly: the crops might be considered a success.   With lightened hearts the Pilgrims now made ready for a "harvest home," the earliest Thanksgiving.

SQUANTUM HEAD.

Squantum is supposed to have been named for Squanto. Squaw Rock, fronting the water at the left, forms, when seen from a certain point, the profile likeness of a squaw.

"Our governor," says Winslow, "sent four men on fowling, that so we might after a special manner rejoice together after we had gathered the fruit of our labors. They four in one day killed as much fowl as, with a little help beside, served the company almost a week."

Wild turkeys, "store of water fowl," and venison were brought in for the feast, and Massasoit and ninety men were entertained at Plymouth for three days, adding as their share five deer, which they gave to the governor, the captain, and others.

The time was passed in out-door sports, — among them the exercise of arms, and, perhaps, trials of skill between the English and the Indians, with fowling-pieces and bows.

The colonists now, writes Governor Bradford, "had all things in good plenty." Each person might draw a peck of corn a week from the common supply, besides being able to find game in abundance for himself.

But the hunting season passed, and thirty·

five new settlers, with nothing to eat and little
to wear, came over from England to be taken
into the colony.

The number to be fed was thus doubled, and
as it was almost impossible to get any large
quantity of corn even from the most friendly
Indians, the settlers soon found themselves
threatened with a famine.

Their provisions might last six months if
doled out in scant measure; so each person was
given but half the usual amount, "which began
to be hard, but they bore it patiently under
hope of supply."

And now the Indians, seeing their distress,
began to menace them. "Yᵉ great people of
yᵉ Narrogansetts, in a braving manner, sente a
messenger unto them with a bundle of arrows
tyed aboute with a great snake-skin;[1] which
their interpreter told them was a threatening
and a challenge. Upon which yᵉ governor . . .
sente them a rounde answer, that if they had
rather have warre than peace, they might begine

[1] The skin of a rattlesnake.

when they would, . . . and by another messenger sent ye snake-skin back with bullets in it."

Canonicus, the sender of the arrows, was terrified by the bullets. He would not touch the snake-skin, nor allow it to stay in his wigwam nor among his people. From one post to another it was hurried, until some one was found bold enough to carry it back to Plymouth.

Though the Narragansetts were cowed by this prompt defiance, the Plymouth men began to fortify their town against attack. " They agreed to inclose their dwellings with a good strong pale, . . . with gates to shut, which were every night locked and a watch kept. . . . This was accomplished very cheerfully, and ye town impaled round by ye beginning of March."

In May and June the Plymouth people were in an almost starving condition. The creeks were full of bass, and the sea of cod, but for lack of proper nets and tackle few of either could be caught.

By July the outlook was rather brighter.

The corn was filling well and the gardens gave fresh vegetables.

But before the month was past, an unruly pack of men, sent out by Thomas Weston, stopped at Plymouth on their way to Massachusetts Bay.

These unexpected guests, sixty in number, not satisfied with their allotted share of food, plundered the ripening cornfields and nearly destroyed the coming harvest. " Much was stolen both by night and day before it became scarce eatable, and much more afterward. And though many were well whipped (when they were taken) for a few ears of corne, yet hunger made others (whom conscience did not restrain) to venture. So as it well appeared y^t famine must still insue ye next year also, if not some way prevented."

During the summer, the colonists, though weak with fasting, succeeded in building a fort.

It was " a large, square house, with a flat roof made of thick-sawn planks, stayed with oak beams"; and stood on the hill, where there had been before only a platform for the guns. Six cannon surmounted the flat roof, while the lower part of the building was used as a church.

A traveller who visited the Pilgrims in 1627 says : —

"They assemble [for church] by beat of drum, each with his musket or firelock, in front of the captain's door : they have their cloaks on and place themselves in order, three abreast, and are led by a sergeant without beat of drum. Behind comes the Governor, in a long robe; beside him on the right hand comes the preacher with his cloak on, and on the left hand the captain with his side arms and cloak on, and with a small cane in his hand; and so they march in good order, and each sets his arms down near him."

In the autumn of 1622 the colonists lost Squanto. At "Manamoycke," or Chatham, whither he had gone with Bradford to get some corn for the famished settlers, he sickened and died, "desiring ye Governor to pray for him, that he might goe to ye Englishman's God in heaven;

and bequeathed sundrie of his things to sundry
of his English friends, as remembrances of his
love; of whom they had a great loss."

Fresh trouble was erelong brought upon
the Pilgrims by Mr. Weston's men, who had
before this left Plymouth to begin their settlement at Wessagusset. These reckless vaga-
bonds, coming to want, fell to robbing the
Indians as they had robbed the Plymouth
folk; until the savages were inflamed with
anger against every white man on the coast.

Standish narrowly escaped being killed.
Having gone to Manomet to fetch more corn,
he was waiting in the wigwam of Canacum for
the shallop to be loaded, when " in came two
of the Massachuset men. The chief of them
was called Wituwamat, a notable insulting
villain. . . . This villain took a dagger from
about his neck . . . and presented it to the
sachem, and after made a long speech . . .
framing it in such sort as the Captain . . . could
not gather anything from it." The speech
was a proposal that Standish should be pres-

ently put to death. Canacum consented, and a fourth Indian, from Pamet, was drawn into the plan.

This man feigned great affection for Captain Standish, " would needs bestow a kettle of some six or seven gallons on him, and would not accept of anything in lieu thereof, saying he was rich, and could afford to bestow such favors on his friends whom he loved. Also he would freely help to carry some of the corn, affirming he had never done the like in his life before." Nor was this enough; finding that for lack of wind Standish must pass the night on shore, he " would needs lodge with him at their rendezvous, having indeed undertaken to kill him before they parted."

The wary captain, however, did not close his eyes. Though he had not understood their words, the actions of the Indians had made him watchful. Restlessly pacing to and fro, or turning one side and then the other toward the fire, for this was in March, and the night was cold, he kept guard until day.

"Why do you not sleep?" asked the Indian; and Standish replied that "he knew not well, but had no desire at all to rest."

The savage, for his part, had no desire at all to attack a waking Englishman, but biding still his time, followed the captain back to Plymouth.

IX.

MASSASOIT'S ILLNESS.

"DURING the time that the captain was at Manomet," writes Edward Winslow, "news came to Plymouth that Massasoit was like to die. . . . Now, it being a commendable manner of the Indians, when any . . . are dangerously sick, for all that profess friendship to them to visit them in their extremity, . . . it was thought meet . . . that as we had ever professed friendship, so we should now maintain the same. . . . To that end, . . . the governor again laid this service upon myself, and fitted me with some cordials to administer to him; having one Master John Hamden ... for my consort and Hobbamock for our guide. So we set forward, and lodged the first night at Namasket where we had friendly entertainment.

"The next day, about one of the clock, we came to a ferry in Corbitant's country,[1] where, upon discharge of my piece, divers Indians came to us from a house not far off. There they told us that Massasoit was dead, and that day buried.... This news struck us blank, but especially Hobbamock, who desired we might return with all speed. I told him I would first think of it. Considering, now, that he being dead, Corbitant was the most likely to succeed him, ... I thought no time so fit as this to enter into more friendly terms with him.... I resolved to put it in practice if Master Hamden and Hobbamock durst attempt it with me, whom I found willing.... So we went towards Mattapoiset [Corbitant's dwelling-place in Swansea].[1]

[1] Probably the same which is now called Slade's Ferry in Swansea. [Young, 315. note.]

"In the way, Hobbamock, manifesting a troubled spirit, broke forth into these speeches: 'Neen womasu Sagimus, neen womasu Sagimus," etc. 'My loving sachim, my loving sachim! Many have I known, but never any like thee;' and, turning to me, he said whilst I lived I should never see his like amongst the Indians. . . . He was no liar; he was not bloody and cruel like other Indians. In anger and passion he was soon reclaimed; easy to be reconciled toward such as had offended him; . . . and that he governed his men better with few strokes than others did with many. . . ."

"At length we came to Mattapoiset,¹ . . . but Corbitant, the sachim, was not at home, but at Pokanoket, which was some five or six miles off. . . . Here we inquired again concerning Massasoit; they thought him dead, but knew no certainty. Whereupon I hired one to go with all expedition to Pokanoket, that we might know the certainty thereof, and, withal, to acquaint Corbitant with our there being.

"About half an hour before sun-setting the

¹ Now Gardner's Neck.

messenger returned, and told us he was not yet dead, though there was no hope we should find him living. Upon this we were much revived, and set forward with all speed, though it was late within night ere we got thither. . . ."

" When we came thither we found the house so full of men as we could scarce get in. . . . There were they in the midst of their charms for him. . . ."

" When they had made an end of their charming, one told him that his friends, the English, were come to see him. Having understanding left, but his sight . . . wholly gone, he asked who was come.

" They told him 'Winsnow,' for they cannot pronounce the letter *l*. . . .

" He desired to speak with me. When I came to him and they told him of it, he put forth his hand to me, which I took.

" Then he said twice, though very inwardly, ' Keen Winsnow?' which is to say, ' Art thou Winslow?'

" I answered, ' Ahhe,' that is, ' Yes.'

" Then he doubled these words ; ' Matta neen wonckanet namen, Winsnow !'

" That is to say, 'O Winslow, I shall never see thee again.'

" Then I called Hobbamock and desired him to tell Massasoit that the governor, hearing of his sickness, was sorry for the same; and though . . . he could not come himself yet he sent me with such things for him as he thought most likely to do him good; . . . whereof if he pleased to take, I would presently give him which he desired; and having a confection of many comfortable conserves, etc., on the point of my knife, I gave him some, which I could scarce get through his teeth. When it was dissolved in his mouth he swallowed the juice of it, whereat those that were about him much rejoiced, saying he had not swallowed anything in two days before. . . .

" Then, he desiring to drink, I dissolved some of it in water and gave him thereof. Within half an hour this wrought a great alteration in him. . . ."

So much better was he that in the middle of the night he asked Winslow to "make him some English pottage, such as he had eaten at Plymouth."

The pottage he wanted was chicken broth, and Winslow promised to shoot some wild fowl next day and make his broth of that. But Massasoit would not wait, and begged Winslow to make him the broth without the fowl. This was a somewhat puzzling task.

"But," says Winslow, "being we must do somewhat, I caused a woman to bruise some corn, and take the flour from it, and set over the grit, or broken corn, in a pipkin, for they have earthen pots of all sizes. When the day broke we went out, it being now March, to seek herbs, but could not find any but strawberry leaves; of which I gathered a handful, and put into the same; and because I had nothing to relish it I went forth again, and pulled up a sassafras root and sliced a piece thereof, and boiled it till it had a good relish, and then took it out again.

"The broth being boiled, I strained it through

my handkerchief and gave him at least a pint,
which he drank and liked it very well.

"After this his sight mended more and more,
. . . insomuch as we with admiration blessed
God for giving his blessing to such raw and
ignorant means. . . .

"Upon his recovery, he brake forth into
these speeches: 'Now I see the English are
my friends and love me; and whilst I live I
will never forget this kindness they have
showed me.'

"In his gratitude he called Hobamok to him
and . . . revealed the plot of the Massachuseuks
. . ."—a plot to kill the white men of Wessagusset and also those of Plymouth.

Massasoit had been asked to join the Massachusetts Indians in this league to destroy the
English, but had refused. He now told Hobamok that if the English wished to save their
colony they must attack and kill the Massachusetts chiefs.

Armed with this advice, Mr. Winslow returned to the settlement.

X.

VICTORY.

THE warning reached Plymouth none too soon. Winslow found Standish on the point of setting off for Massachusetts, still attended by that loving Pamet Indian.

The journey was postponed, and the Indian quietly dismissed. Then the matter was laid before the council.

The council decided that Massasoit must be obeyed. Standish must suddenly fall upon the Indian leaders and destroy them.

With eight men, therefore, — he refused to take more, — Captain Standish sailed to Massachusetts Bay. Arriving at Wessagusset, where the trouble was expected to begin, he found that many of the miserable settlers there had already "starved and died with cold and hunger." Others, "so base were they, became servants to the Indians, and would cutt them woode and fetch them water for a cap full of corne." One, "in gathering shell-fish was so weake as he stuck fast in ye mudd, and was found dead in ye place," and most of them had "left their dwellings and scattered up and down in ye woods and by ye watersides, — where they could find groundnuts and clams."

The Indians had ceased to fear or respect them. "Many times, as they lay thus scattered abroad, and had set on a pot with groundnuts or shell-fish, when it was ready the Indians would come and eat it up; and when night came, whereas some of them had a sorry blanket, or such like, to lappe themselves in, the Indians would take it and let ye other lye all night in the cold."

Standish did what he could to rally their feeble courage. He tried to induce them to come back to their village, promised each man a pint a day from the slender store of seed-corn, and offered shelter to any who wished to return to Plymouth.

While he was busied with these affairs and awaiting a chance for action, the savages tried to discover the reason for his visit.

They first sent a scout to Wessagusset, with furs to sell to the English. Standish carried on the trading with outward smoothness; but the Indian returned to his friends, saying that "he could see by the captain's eyes that he was angry in his heart."

Pecksuot appeared next, and said to Hobamok apart:—

"The captain has come to kill us: tell him we know it, but fear him not; neither will we shun him; but let him begin when he dare, he shall not take us at unawares."

Then came Wituwamat, whetting his knife. On its handle was pictured a woman's face. "Hinnaim namen, hinnaim michen, matta cuts," said Wituwamat. "By and by it shall see and by and by it shall eat, but not speak!"

Pecksuot boasted further, and this time to Standish himself: "Though you are a great captain, you are but a little man. I am no sachem, yet I am a man of great strength and courage."

Standish made no answer to his taunt; but

the next day, when Pecksuot, Wituwamat,
Wituwamat's brother, and another Indian were
together in the room with him, — three or
four other white men being present, — he gave
a sudden signal, which his friends well understood.

In an instant they made fast the door. Standish then sprang upon Pecksuot, and, "snatching his own knife from his neck, though with
much struggling, killed him therewith; the
point whereof he had made as sharp as a
needle, and ground the back to an edge."
The rest at the same time overcame Wituwamat and the other Indians, and the combat
ended.

Hobamok took no part in the affray. Standing aside, he watched the captain's terrible
hand-to-hand struggle, then, smiling, turned
to him with these words : "Yesterday, Pecksuot, bragging of his own strength and stature,
said, though you were a great captain, yet you
were but a little man; but to-day I see you
are big enough to lay him on the ground."

Three more Indians were afterward killed, one by Standish's party, and two by the Wessa-gusset men. Fifteen of the natives, also, whom the English saw filing through the woods, were chased away; Hobamok this time stripping off his coat and pursuing them hotly. Then the captain, taking with him those of the Wessa-gusset colony who wished to remain in the country, returned to Plymouth.

He had done enough. A panic seized the savages. Not knowing where else the English might strike, they fled from their wigwams into swamps and forest fastnesses, where they lived for a while in terror, until, seized by colds or fevers, many of them died. Canacum of Mano-met, Aspinet of Nauset, and Iyanough perished in this way.

In April, "when the leaves of the white oak were as big as the ear of a mouse," came the planting time. The Pilgrims therefore, gladly setting aside their fears of war, gave their attention to the fields.

A greater quantity of corn than they had

attempted to raise before was to be put into
the ground this year; and the settlers resolved
to try another plan of work. Heretofore the
cornfields had been common property, the
work and the harvest had been shared alike
by all; but now each family was to have the
care of its own cornfield, and enjoy the use
of its own grain.

The wisdom of this plan was soon shown.
The women, now, and even the children, helped
hoe the home corn-patch, and the labor went
on with a heartier will.

The young corn came up well; but "six
weeks after the latter setting, there scarce fell
any rain, so that the stalk of that which was first
set began to send forth the ear before it came
to half growth, and that which was later not
like to yield any at all, both blade and stalk
hanging the head and changing the color in
such a manner as we judged it utterly dead. . . .
Now were our hopes overthrown and we discouraged, our joy being turned into mourning."

In their distress they appointed a day for
prayer.

"A day was ... set apart from all other employments, hoping that the same God which had stirred us up hereunto, would be moved hereby in mercy to look down upon us, and grant the request of our dejected souls. . . . But O, the mercy of our God! who was as ready to hear as we to ask; for though in the morning, when we assembled together, the heavens were as clear, and the drought as like to continue as ever it was, yet, (our exercise continuing some eight or nine hours,) before our departure, the weather was overcast, the clouds gathered together on all sides, and on the next morning distilled such soft, sweet and moderate showers of rain, continuing some fourteen days, and mixed with such seasonable weather as it was hard to say whether our withered corn or drooping affections were most quickened or revived; such was the bounty and goodness of our God."

Though courage had returned to them with the recovery of the crops, many weeks must pass before the ripening of the harvest, and the colonists were still "in a very low condition." Clothing as well as food was sorely needed, — "many were ragged in apparel, and some little better than half naked."

In good time, however, the Anne and Little James arrived from England with supplies. Besides supplies, the vessels brought welcome additions to the colony; among them were William Brewster's wife with her daughters, Fear and Patience; a certain Barbara who afterward became Barbara Standish; and Mistress Alice Southworth, whom William Bradford had long known and whom he was now to marry.

Not much had the Plymouth people to offer their guests. "The best dish they could present their friends with was a lobster or a piece of fish, without bread or anything else but a cupp of fair spring water." Bradford tells us that the passengers, on seeing the want and poverty of the settlers, were "much daunted and dismayed, . . . some wished themselves in England againe; others fell a-weeping, fancying their own misery in what y^{ey} saw now in others; other some pitying the distress they saw their friends had long been in and were still under; in a word, all were full of sadness. Only, some of their old friends,"—does not this hint that Mistress Southworth was of a cheerful temper?—"rejoiced to see them, and y^t it was no worse with them, for they could not expect it should be better, and now hoped they should enjoy better days together."

The hope was fulfilled. By autumn "ye effect of their particular planting was well seene; for all had, one way and other, pretty well to bring ye year aboute, and some of ye abler sortes . . . had to spare and sell to others, so as any general want or famine hath not been amongst them to this day." Their worst trials were past. Success was assured; and a foot-hold won for the new nation that was to grow from their dauntless determination and faith.

"God gave them plenty, and ye face of things was changed, to ye rejoicing of ye hearts of many, for which they blessed God."

BOSTON IN ENGLAND.

Two brothers, of a noble family, one called Adulph, the other Botolph, were born in England, in the seventh century.

They were sent to Belgic France to be educated, and in time became two learned monks. The king of France gave Adulph a post of honor in Belgium, but Botolph went back to England to found a monastery there.

Though offered his choice of all the rich farm lands of southeastern Britain, the good St. Botolph, unwilling to disturb any homesteads, selected "a wild region not inhabited by men, but only by devils"—"a certain untilled place where none dwelt, named Ikanho." At Icanoe the monastery was raised; and St. Botolph lived in it with his followers to the end of his peaceful days.

He was a kindly, helpful man throughout his life; and after his death the mariners consid-

ST. BOTOLPH'S CHURCH

ered him their patron saint. His name itself meant bot-holp, or boat help; and seamen or vessels in distress were supposed to be under his care.

At the end of a hundred years, the monastery was destroyed by the Danes. But the memory of St. Botolph lived; and a settlement which replaced the monastery took his name. It was called the town of St. Botolph, or Botolph's-town.

With centuries of use the word Botolph's-town became softened to Botolston, and Botoston, and Boston; and now the name of the city bears little likeness to that of the monk.

In 1309 the corner-stone of a beautiful great church, named St. Botolph's church, was laid in Boston; and in King James's time, when the church had long been finished, Mr. John Cotton was made its pastor.

When Mr. Cotton had preached in the church about three years he became a Puritan and a Non-conformist; and all his people turned Puritans and Non-conformists too.

Mr. Isaac Johnson and his wife, the Lady Arbella, were among Mr. Cotton's hearers; and a Mr. John Winthrop, of whom we shall learn more, also knew Mr. Cotton and valued him.

In 1630 Mr. Johnson, Lady Arbella, Mr. Winthrop, and others, disheartened by the state of affairs in England and in the church, set sail for America.

Two years later, Mr. Cotton was driven from his pulpit. It was in this way: "A ... fellow in the town, who had been punished by the magistrates," vented his rage by informing the High Commission Court that "the magistrates [of Boston] did not kneel" at a certain part of the service.

The persons to whom he told this asked for the name of the minister of the Boston church.

"'Nay,' said he, 'the minister is an honest man, and never did me any wrong.'"

They insisted, however, and he was forced to confess that it was John Cotton.

Upon this, Mr. Cotton was summoned to appear before the High Commission Court; but knowing that if he appeared he would be thrown into prison, Mr. Cotton hid himself, and begged the Earl of Dorset to plead his cause.

The earl tried to help him, but in vain, and at last sent word that had the charge been of drunkenness, or bad conduct, or "'any such lesser fault,'" forgiveness might have been granted, but "'inasmuch as he had been guilty of Non-conformity and Puritanism the crime was unpardonable; and therefore,' said he, 'you must fly for your safety.'"

Mr. Cotton, finding that he must leave England, travelled to London in disguise; and sailed thence to the new Boston which Mr. Winthrop and other Puritans had founded in America.

Many vicars have preached in the carved pulpit of St. Botolph's church since Mr. Cotton's day, but none have been so famous as Mr. Cotton. In the meantime, though the younger city on our side of the Atlantic has far out-stripped the town for which it was named, to this day it contains nothing half so grand as the huge church tower of old Boston.

I.

WILLIAM BLACKSTONE was the first white man to settle upon the land now covered by the city of Boston. No city stood here when he came; the whole place was a wild, uneven patch of hills and hollows.

He was an Englishman, and had been a clergyman. He left England, so he said, because he "did not like the Lord-Bishops." The king and bishops of England wished to be obeyed in all church matters: a great number of Englishmen found that they could not obey the king and bishops; and many of them came, as Mr. Blackstone did, to America.

We cannot find out just when Mr. Blackstone crossed the ocean: it may have been in 1623. In 1625 or 1626 he had already arrived, with leave to claim fifty acres of land, and had

chosen for his own a part of this hilly peninsula which the Indians called Shawmut.

Boston children know the hill on which the
State House stands. It is a simple, round-
topped hill now; but then it had three peaks,
— one where the State House is, one near
Pemberton Square, and one upon the west,
along Mt. Vernon Street.

Mr. Blackstone made the sunny slope of the
western peak his dwelling-place. His house,
and a spring from which he drew clear cold
water, were, it is thought, somewhere within
the space enclosed by Beacon Street, Spruce
Street, Pinckney Street, and the water. A
point not far from his cottage came to be
called Blackstone's Point: we think it was
the one which once jutted out into the river
at the foot of Pinckney Street.

Having built his house, Mr. Blackstone dug
and planted a garden. He set out an apple
orchard too, — the first ever started here.

No wife, no child, no friend, shared his home.
In all Shawmut there was no other house.

He lived alone, and seemed to wish to live so. He has been called a hermit, a solitary, a recluse.

His nearest neighbor lived across the river north of Shawmut. A house stood on Noddle's Island, or East Boston; another on Thompson's Island, in the harbor. Two or three small settlements had been made upon the coast, and far away was the Plymouth Colony; but most of the Massachusetts shore was a waste of woodlands and marshes, with no white men to be seen for miles and miles, and only here and there a village of the Indians.

For three or four years Mr. Blackstone tended his orchard and garden, while little happened around him, save the passing from spring and summer to autumn and winter, and from winter back to spring again. He had brought some books with him from England, — one hundred and eighty-six volumes, — and these were his chief delight. He was so fond of reading that he was called not only a recluse, but a " bookish man." Through the

long, silent winters his books must have
seemed to him like real friends.

At the end of the three or four years a few
other white men from Salem, which had grown
up meanwhile, found their way to the river's
northern edge, and settled there, building several houses, — one of which was quite large,
and was called the " Great House." Charlestown was the name given to this little settlement: Charles the First was King of England
at that time, and the town and our river were
both named for him.

About a year after the building of the Great
House, a larger company of men came to
Charlestown. Their leader was John Winthrop, who had been made governor of the
whole Massachusetts colony,— Salem, Charlestown, Shawmut, and all.

Mr. Blackstone soon learned that Governor
Winthrop's company were in much distress.
Many of them had fallen ill ; some had died.
One cause of their trouble was that they had
not been able to find good water in Charles-

town. The only spring they knew of could not be reached except at low tide, and its water was brackish, unfit to drink.

Living alone had not made Mr. Blackstone a bad neighbor. He knew that in Shawmut water was plenty, and that the settlers would thrive far better there than in Charlestown. He went to Governor Winthrop, told him of a certain " very excellent spring" in the eastern part of Shawmut, and urged him to leave Charlestown and settle in Shawmut instead.

Governor Winthrop did leave Charlestown, and did settle in Shawmut. The once quiet place became alive with hurrying workers. Houses were built, streets were laid out, a town sprang up upon the shore. The town was named Boston.

It was one of the rules of the colony that only members of the church could be allowed to vote or take part in public affairs. A man who did not belong to the church was not counted a " freeman" of the colony.

Now, William Blackstone did not wish to

belong to the church.   He did not like the church ways of the Boston men any better than he had liked the church ways of the English bishops.

Since he would not join the church, he soon felt ill at ease as a member of the town. The rigid rules of the new-comers fretted him; their active life destroyed the comfort of his home. With tastes and wishes unlike those of his near neighbors, he was out of place among them, — a stranger, though on his own soil.   He must have felt, then, a loneliness which had not come to him while living apart from other men.   He decided that he must go away.

He sold to the town most of his land, — all of it except the six acres on which were his house, his garden, and his orchard.   This six-acre lot he kept for some time longer, though he never lived upon it again.

Part of the land bought from him was used by the townsfolk as a training-field, and as a common where all might pasture their cows:

that very land is our Common still, though it is hardly a pasture-ground now.

With a portion of the money received for his land, Mr. Blackstone furnished himself with "a stock of cows," and, taking them with him, started upon a southward journey.

To the men of the town he said: "I came from England because I did not like the Lord-Bishops; but I cannot join with you, because I would not be under the Lord-Brethren!"

II.

MR. BLACKSTONE'S way lay through forests and across streams. No road ran broad and smooth before him. No bridges led him dry-shod over the water-courses. His path, at best, must have been an Indian trail, winding toward shallow fords, or where great rocks made stepping-stones from shore to shore.

Did he have an Indian guide? Did he go

afoot? Did he take his books with him then, or send for them later? How were they carried, — by Indians or by one of the few horses brought from England?

Among his books Mr. Blackstone had some papers which we think might have answered questions like these; but the papers and books were all burned not long after Mr. Blackstone's death, and we shall never know what they may have had to tell of his life in England and in this country.

The journey was brought to an end at about forty miles from Boston, beside a narrow river in a lovely fertile valley.

On the eastern bank of the river Mr. Blackstone found a meadow which rose in three stretches, like three long, wide steps, each higher than the last. On the first of these he built a house; on the second he dug a well. A new garden grew here under his care; so did a new apple-orchard. The place came to be known as Rehoboth, and the river was named for him, — the Blackstone. That part

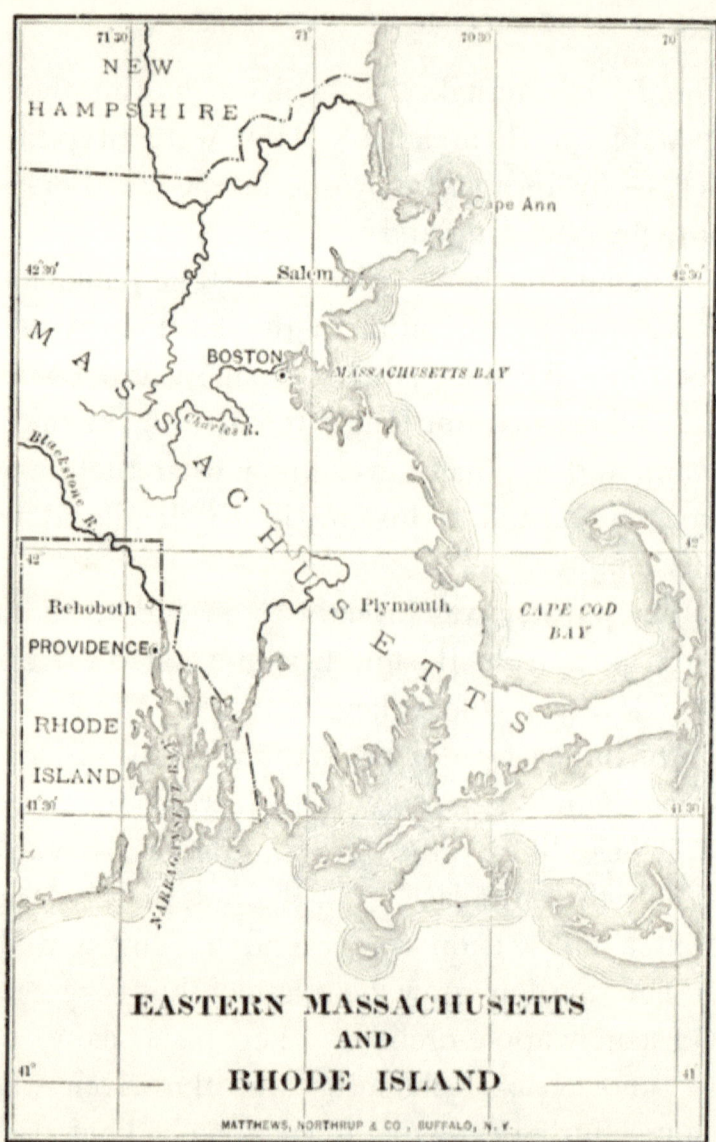

EASTERN MASSACHUSETTS
AND
RHODE ISLAND

MATTHEWS, NORTHRUP & CO., BUFFALO, N.Y.

of Rehoboth is Lonsdale now, but the river still holds its old name.

At Rehoboth Mr. Blackstone again led a hermit's life. Here he was even farther away from other men than he had been at Shawmut.

He found the new home much to his liking. At the west of his house, rising steeply from the meadow and close upon the river's brink, was a hillock sixty or seventy feet high. Mr. Blackstone used to read or study upon this knoll, and he named it Study Hill. He was still a "bookish" man.

After about a year the town of Providence grew up, seven miles away from Rehoboth; but the Providence people did not disturb Mr. Blackstone. Indeed, he must have enjoyed having them near, as he sometimes preached in Providence for Roger Williams, the founder of the town. He seems to have been fond of the children and young people of Providence: he used to carry apples to them from Rehoboth; and many of the children, born in America, had perhaps never tasted apples before. His orchard was a famous one. An old account, speaking of his apples, says: " He had the first of the sort . . . called yellow sweetings that were ever in the world."

More than once, while living at Rehoboth, Mr. Blackstone visited his old home in Boston. Boston grew rapidly from year to year. The six-acre lot was sold, and several houses were built upon it. In one of these houses lived a Mistress Anne Pollard. She has said that Mr. Blackstone sometimes stopped at her house.

After living twenty-four years at Rehoboth, Mr. Blackstone married a Boston woman, a Mrs. Martha Stevenson, and took her back to Rehoboth with him. Their wedding-day fell upon a Fourth of July, and Mr. Blackstone made holiday every time the day came round. He could not guess that by-and-by a whole new nation would be greeting the Fourth of July as its Independence Day.

As Mr. Blackstone grew older, he found the walk from Rehoboth to Providence rather long. He had no horse: what should he do? Among his cattle was a young bull; this he trained to obey him. When it had become strong enough, he taught it to carry him upon its back. Here was a steed! After that, on Sunday mornings, Mr. Blackstone walked to Providence no more. With his sermons or his apples, or with both, he mounted his bull, and was taken safely, if not swiftly, to town. It would be an odd sight now, but it was not so uncommon in those days.

A son was born in Rehoboth, and Mr. Blackstone spent the rest of his life there. About a month after his death a war, called King Philip's War, broke out between the white men and some of the Indians; and a party of Indians, coming to Rehoboth, set fire to Mr. Blackstone's house and burned or carried off everything in it. If only the books and papers might have been saved!

The stones of the well were to be seen for some years after; and fifty years ago some feeble old apple-trees were still there, and still bearing fruit. They were thought to have grown from shoots of Mr. Blackstone's trees.

The place is greatly changed now. Railroad-tracks and telegraph wires pass through Study Hill; and if we should go to the spot to-day, we should see, near where Mr. Blackstone's house once stood, the Lonsdale railway station.

JOHN WINTHROP.

1630.

I.

On a day in March, in the year 1630, a good ship rode at anchor off the English shore.

She bore a company of English Puritans who were bidding good-by to old England and turning their faces toward a new country far beyond sight in the west.

Puritans fared badly in England in those days. Their church services and church beliefs were not quite like those of the king and bishops, and this so displeased the king and bishops that Puritan meetings were forbidden, and Puritan preachers driven from their pulpits.

For the sake of being free to worship God in the way they thought right, these Puritans were setting forth to plant their church over

seas, in America.   Their chief man was John
Winthrop; he was to be their governor.

The ship lay near Cowes, waiting for the
wind to veer.   Day after day she rocked there,
while gusts swept down upon her from the
west or southwest, and rain fell upon her
deck.   Stormy March would not let her go.

Some of the people on board of her came
from the English town of Boston, among them
Mr. Isaac Johnson and his wife, the lady
Arbella.

Lady Arbella was an earl's daughter, and
one who had never suffered hardship.   She
found herself now, not in a fine, roomy steamer
like that in which we should cross the Atlantic,
but crowded into close quarters on a little
pitching vessel, with poor food and stifling air.

She must have grown very tired of the ship
even before it put out to sea.   We are glad
to read in Governor Winthrop's journal, begun
at Cowes, that "the lady Arbella and the gen-
tlewomen and Mr. Johnson and some others
went on shore to refresh themselves."

JOHN WINTHROP.

Lady Arbella's name came first in whatever Governor Winthrop wrote about the women of the company, and her comfort was the first to be cared for whenever comfort could be thought of at all.

Every one must have wished to serve the gentle and delicate lady; the ship itself took on a new name for her. It became the "Arbella" in her honor.

Three other ships were ready to sail with Governor Winthrop's vessel; seven more were to follow. Governor Winthrop had with him on board the "Arbella" two young sons,— Stephen Winthrop, a boy twelve years old, and Adam, who was only ten. An older son, Henry, followed in one of the other ships. Governor Winthrop's wife and the rest of his family did not leave England until nearly a year later.

For a whole week the "Arbella" waited at Cowes; for another week she was anchored near Yarmouth, then, on Thursday, the 8th of April, "about six in the morning, the wind

being E. and N., and fair weather," she
" weighed anchor and set sail."

The captain of the "Arbella" had been told
at Yarmouth that some Spanish vessels were
lying in wait for his fleet. England and Spain
were at war then, and English vessels were
very likely to meet with trouble from Spaniards upon the sea.

On the morning of their second day from
Yarmouth eight vessels were seen astern of
them. The captain feared that they might be
enemies. To put the "Arbella" in fighting
order he " caused the gun-room and gun-deck
to be cleared," all the hammocks to be taken
down, the guns to be loaded, and powder-chests
and fireworks to be made ready.

" After noon," the journal goes on to say,
" we still saw those eight ships to stand towards
us. Having more wind than we, they came
up apace . . . whereupon we all prepared to
fight with them, and took down some cabins
which were in the way of our ordnance, and
out of every ship were thrown such bed matters

as were subject to take fire, . . . and drew forth
our men and armed them with muskets and
other weapons and instruments for fireworks,
and for an experiment our captain shot a ball
of wildfire fastened to an arrow, out of a cross-
bow, which burnt in the water a good time.
The lady Arbella and the other women and
children were removed into the lower deck that
they might be out of danger. All things being
thus fitted, we went to prayer upon the upper
deck. It was much to see how cheerful and
comfortable all the company appeared; not a
woman or child that shewed fear. . . .

"It was now about one of the clock, and the
fleet seemed to be within a league of us; therefore our captain, because he would shew he
was not afraid of them, and that he might
see the issue before night should overtake us,
tacked about and stood to meet them, and when
we came near we perceived them to be our
friends. . . . So when we drew near, every ship
(as they met) saluted each other and the musketeers discharged their small shot; and so

God be praised, our fear and danger was turned
into mirth and friendly entertainment.

"Our danger being thus over, we espied two
boats on fishing in the channel; so every of
our four ships manned out a skiff, and we
bought of them great store of excellent fresh
fish of divers sorts."

The children of the ship, and a number of
the grown people too, were seasick for a time.
They lay in the close cabin in a very unhappy
state. One day, when they had begun to feel
better, Governor Winthrop sent for them to
come on deck. They dragged themselves up,
though some of them were hardly able to
crawl. A rope was then stretched along the
deck, and they were made to stand, "some of
one side, and some of the other, and sway it
up and down till they were warm, and by this
means they soon grew well and merry."

Upon the next rough day some were sick, as
before; but Governor Winthrop wrote: "Such
as came up upon the deck, and stirred themselves, were presently well again. Therefore

our captain set our children and young men to some harmless exercises, which the seamen were very active in, and did our people much good, though they would sometimes play the wags with them."

Too much playing the wag would have been quickly checked. Puritan children were taught that they should be seen, not heard. Puritan young folks were led in staid and serious ways. Puritan men and women were grave, even stern. They had seen a great deal of folly and sin among a light-hearted set of people in England. They were so bent on keeping their children from folly and sin that they sometimes kept them from light-heartedness as well.

We cross the ocean now in nine, eight, seven days. Governor Winthrop was seventy-six days in crossing.[1] He was at sea through all of April, through all of May; and not until the 6th of June did he come in sight of land. On the 8th, these land-hungry voyagers caught a glimpse of the beautiful hills of Mount Desert, blue, serene, stately, in the distance.

[1] Leaving Cowes March 29, anchoring at Salem June 12.

The journey had been most wearisome.
Storm after storm had beaten upon the vessel;
the people, cramped in narrow space, had suffered for want of exercise. Their diet of salted
meats had caused an illness among them. They
longed for the wide green reaches of the solid
earth.

Rejoice with them, for here Governor Winthrop could write: " We had now fair sunshine
weather, and so pleasant a sweet air as did much
refresh us, and there came a smell off the shore
like the smell of a garden. There came a wild
pigeon into our ship, and another small land
bird."

Four days after that the "Arbella" came to
anchor in Salem Harbor.

Salem was a half-starved little settlement,
held to its high courage by a few brave men.
Its people looked eagerly for the coming of the
ships, and, though food for their own daily
needs was far from plentiful, they had tasked
their larders to the uttermost to provide good
cheer for their guests. A supper was prepared

WINTHROP'S FLEET.

on shore, — "a good supper," writes Governor Winthrop, "of venison pasty."

The pasty was not for the whole ship's company; but those who were not asked to the supper found another feast spread for them in the kindly fields. Ripe and red it glowed under its cool, dark leaves. What a sight for sea-parched men! Governor Winthrop, after telling us of the pasty, writes: "In the mean time most of our people went on shore upon the land of Cape Ann, which lay very near us, and gathered store of fine strawberries."

That same day Stephen and Adam Winthrop had their first sight of a red man; for an Indian paddled his canoe to the ship's side, and, coming aboard, slept there all night.

All this fell on a Saturday. The passengers remained upon the "Arbella" until Monday. Then, leaving the ship, while its guns bade them a loud farewell, they took up their abode for a while in Salem.

II.

"SALEM, where wee landed, pleased us not," wrote Mr. Dudley to the Countess of Lincoln, sister-in-law of the Lady Arbella.

Since they did not care to remain in Salem Governor Winthrop and others set about finding a better site for the town they wished to build. The journal says, "We went to Mattachusetts to find out a place for our sitting down."

Mattachusetts, Masachulets, Messatsoosec, Massachusetts,[1] — the word was spelled in many ways, — meant then only the land near Boston Harbor. Salem and Plymouth were quite outside of the Massachusetts of those days.

---

[1] Messatsoosec or Massachusetts, it is thought, was the Indian name given to a hillock on the shore of Quincy Bay. We know that it was also given to the hilly land near the mouth of Charles River, and to the Indian tribe dwelling in this part of the country. Part of Quincy was known as the Massachusetts Fields, and Blue Hill once was called Massachusetts Mount.

Governor Winthrop visited Charlestown and Noddle's Island,[1] and went six miles up the Mystic River. He also found his way to the small settlement at Nantasket. Returning, he advised the company to remove to Charlestown.

Trouble was beginning to press heavily upon them. The sick did not revive, grumblers made bitter complaints, the weak-hearted would gladly have gone back to England. Governor Winthrop's hope and cheer did not forsake him, though these murmurings came to his ears at a time when he had his special grief to bear. This special grief was the death of his son Henry.

Henry Winthrop arrived in Salem soon after his father's return from Massachusetts. On the very day of landing he started, with two or three of the ship's officers, to see some Indian wigwams not far away. "They saw, on the other side of the river, a small canoe. He would have had one of the company swim over and fetch it, rather than walk several miles on foot.

[1] East Boston.

it being very hot weather, but none of the
party could swim but himself; and so he
plunged in, and, as he was swimming over, was
taken with the cramp a few roods from shore,
and drowned."

"My son Henry! my son Henry!" wrote
Governor Winthrop to his wife. "Ah, poor
child! Yet it grieves me much more for my
dear daughter.[1] . . . Yet for all these things
(I praise my God) I am not discouraged."

He was not discouraged. There was dis-
couragement enough among his people. They
looked to him for strength. He laid his bur-
den aside, that he might help them in bearing
theirs.

The company left Salem for Charlestown,
but their suffering did not cease.

Charlestown had not shelter for so many
homeless folk. Governor Winthrop and others
of the foremost men used the "Great House,"
which had been put up the year before; and
"the multitude set up cottages, tents and

---

[1] Henry's wife in England.

booths about the Town Hill."[1] Samuel Green,
the printer, who came from England in the ship
with Mr. Dudley, was one of those who had not
even a tent to sleep in. Long afterward, when
he had a very good roof, not only for himself
but for his family, he used to tell his children
that when he first came ashore he and several
others were glad to lodge at night in an empty
cask!

It was a life that none but the strongest
could endure. The sick sank under it; num-
bers of them died. Read this, written by one
who saw it all himself: "Almost in every family . . . mourning and woe was heard, and no
fresh food to be had to cherish them. . . .
And that which added to their present distress
was the want of fresh water; for although the
place did afford plenty, yet for the present they
could find but one spring and that not to be
come at but when the tide was downe."[2]

Lady Arbella was not even well enough to
get to Charlestown. She lingered in Salem,

---

[1] Town Records.   [2] Edward Johnson.

and before long "left that wilderness for the
heavenly paradise."[1]   "She took New England
in her way to heaven."[1]

Looking south across the river, Governor
Winthrop and his people could see a three-
peaked hill rising from a peninsula upon the
further shore.

The Indian name for the peninsula was
Shawmut, but the Charlestown folk called it
Tri-mountain, for its triple hill.

Tri-mountain had upon it one small cottage,
in which lived Mr. William Blackstone,—a man
who seemed to care for books and solitude more
than for anything else in the world.   He owned
about one fifteenth of Tri-mountain, or Shawmut,
and had there a garden, a spring, and an orchard.

His spring was not the only one upon the
place; Tri-mountain abounded in springs; one
of the best was upon the eastern shore.

"Mr. Blackstone," say the Charlestown Records, "dwelling on the other side Charles River,
alone, at a place by the Indians called Shaw-

---

[1] Cotton Mather.

mut, where he only had a cottage, at or not far off the place called Blackstone's Point, he came and acquaint the governor of an excellent spring there, withal inviting and soliciting him thither."

Governor Winthrop thought well of Mr. Blackstone's invitation; he decided to take up his abode near the "Great Spring," which was where our post-office now stands.

Through the summer, some at one time some at another, most of the company crossed to Tri-mountain and settled themselves in their new homes. One of the first boats touching at the Shawmut side of the river carried a lively young woman named Anne, who, "being at that time but a romping girl," sprang from the boat declaring that she would be the first to land. She was not only first among her companions in stepping ashore, but first among all white women in treading Boston soil; no woman of her race had set foot here before.

Anne Pollard's life was a very long one; she lived to be one hundred and five years old.

Her account of certain matters which no one
else was old enough or clear-headed enough
to remember is of service still. She has said
that our hills were covered with blueberry
and other bushes, and that the whole place
was very uneven, abounding in swamps and
hollows.

Governor Winthrop did not leave Charlestown until the middle or latter part of the autumn; then his house, the frame of which was
already begun, was carried across the river.
The Old South Church, on Washington Street,
stands upon what was once Governor Winthrop's garden. Mr. Isaac Johnson's land
was where King's Chapel is now. Mr. Johnson did not live to build upon his land: he
died in Charlestown, and the lot became his
burial-place; it is the oldest burial-ground in
Boston.

"About two in the morning Mr. Isaac Johnson died; his wife, the lady Arbella, of the
house of Lincoln, being dead about one month
before. He was a holy man and wise, and died

in sweet peace, leaving some part of his substance to the colony."

The Charlestown Records go on to tell us
that "After the death of Mr. Johnson and
divers others, the Governor, with Mr. Wilson,
and the greater part of the church removed
thither: whither also the frame of the Governor's house in preparation at this time was . . .
carried; when people began to build their
houses against winter; and this place was
called Boston.

III.

GOVERNOR WINTHROP, when settled in his Boston home, wrote: "My dear wife, we are here in a paradise. Though we have not beef and mutton, &c., yet (God be praised) we want them not; our Indian corn answers for all."

Their Indian corn, alas, soon became scarce; in place of meal the women learned to make a poor kind of flour from acorns, and the children were glad to dig clams and mussels to eke out their scanty dinners.

The ship "Lyon" had long ago been sent to England for fresh supplies; but week after week, month after month went by, and still she did not return.

Winter soon closed in upon them; winter, fiercer, drearier than our winters usually are, — colder far than any they had known in England. Snow covered the ground-nuts and acorns, ice held fast the clams; the corn was nearly gone. "People were very much tired and discouraged," say the Charlestown Records, "especially when they heard that the Governor himself had the last batch of bread in the oven."

We read that at the very time when that last batch of bread was in the oven a man came to Governor Winthrop to beg some meal. The little that was left was promptly given, and — wonderful! — that same day the ship arrived. Cotton Mather tells the story: "On February 5th, . . . when he was distributing the last handful of meal in the barrel unto a poor man distressed by the 'wolf at the door,' at that instant they spied a ship arrived at the harbour's mouth, laden with provisions for them all."

The ship at the harbor's mouth was the "Lyon;" hunger was past, and a Thanksgiving Day was kept with rejoicing by all plantations. "We held a day of thanksgiving, for this ship's arrival," says the journal, and gives the date, — the 22d of February, 1631.[1] This was Boston's first Thanksgiving Day. Salem had had one in July, after the safe arrival of the

[1] On the 22d of February, 1732, George Washington was born.

ships.   Plymouth had had a famous one ten
years before, in November, after the gathering-in
of her first harvest; and this Plymouth Thanksgiving Day we celebrate yearly.

In the spring the settlers planted many an
acre of pease, beans, and corn.   No other winter should find them waiting for ships to bring
them food.   The cornfields on the slope of the
southernmost hill gave the hill a short-lived
name, — the " Corn-hill," people called it.   A
fort soon took the place of the corn, and the
hill became Fort Hill instead.   The fort has
gone, the hill has been cut away; and where
they once were we have only Fort Square.

The country at the south of Boston was
given the name " Rocksbury," for its pudding-
stone ledges.   Wolves prowled there, and Indians were not far away.   To keep out wolves
and Indians the Boston folk built a wall on
the narrow neck between their town and Rox-
bury; and an officer and six men lived by the
wall as a constant guard.   It was quite near
the place where Dover Street is now.

A sentry was posted on the Treamount's highest peak; later, a beacon was raised there, —a tall, stout mast with an arm atop, and a great kettle of tar at the end of the arm. This hill had two names, — Sentry Hill in the sentry's time, and Beacon Hill since.

The Indians, after all, gave the town no trouble; they were always friendly to Governor Winthrop.

Many of the Indians who had lived near the coast had been killed by a great plague which had swept through their country some years before; those who were spared by the plague had been weakened by wars. The Massachusetts tribe, once large and powerful, was now made up of a very few families, led by a chief called Chick-a-tau-bot, "House-a-fire," who was himself ruled by a greater chief named Massasoit.

Chickataubot had seen the "white birds" of the pale-faces come flying across the water to his shore, had watched the building of the white men's wigwams, had touched the soft,

warm garments of the strangers, and listened
to the thunder which they carried in their
hands.   He wished to make them his allies.

Leaving his home in Neponset, he went, with
a band of his people, both men and women, to
Governor Winthrop's house in Boston, and
there, with his politest words and gestures,
offered a gift, — a hogshead of corn.   Read the
journal : " Chickatabot came with his sannops
and squaws, and presented the governour with
a hogshead of Indian corn."

The Governor took the corn, thanked Chickataubot, and invited him and all who were with
him to sit and eat.   They did so, and then
began to think of going home.   By this time
great clouds had rolled over the sky, and a
thunder-storm had begun.   Governor Winthrop
asked his guests to remain ; but Chickataubot
knew that his people could not long be pleasant
inmates of an English house, and wisely sent
them off in the midst of the storm, though he
himself and one brave and a squaw did stay
all night.   " The next day after dinner he re-

turned home, the governour giving him cheese and peas and a mug and some other small things."

About three weeks after this, the journal tells us, "Chickatabot came to the governour and desired to buy some English clothes for himself. The governour told him, that English sagamores did not use to truck; but he called his tailor and gave him order to make him a suit of clothes; whereupon he gave the governour two large skins of coat beaver, and, after he and his men had dined, they departed, and said he would come again three days after for his suit."

He did not fail to come. "Chickatabot came to the governour again, and he put him into a very good new suit from head to foot, and after he set meat before them; but he would not eat till the governour had given thanks, and after meat he desired him to do the like, and so departed."

Wolves were nearly as plenty as Indians, and could not so easily be turned into friends. Govcrnor Winthrop's farm[1] on the Mystic suffered from them. One evening, "The governour, being at his farm-house at Mistick, walked out after supper and took a piece in his hand, supposing he might see a wolf (for they came daily about the house, and killed swine and calves, &c.); and, being about half a mile off, it grew suddenly dark, so as in coming home, he mistook his path, and went till he came to a little house of Sagamore John,[2] which stood empty. There he stayed, and having a piece of match in his pocket (for he always carried about him match and a compass, and in summer time snakeweed) he made a good fire near the house, and lay down upon some old mats, which he found there, and so spent the night, sometimes walking by the fire, sometimes singing psalms, and sometimes getting wood, but could not sleep. It was (through God's mercy) a warm night;

[1] Called "Ten Hills Farm" because ten hills could be counted around it. It was nearly opposite the entrance to Malden River.

[2] Sagamore John was an Indian. Indians often had several lodges in different parts of the forest, and slept in the nearest when out hunting.

but a little before day it began to rain, and,
having no cloak, he made shift by a long pole
to climb up into the house. In the morning,
there came thither an Indian squaw, but per-
ceiving her before she had opened the door, he
barred her out; yet she stayed there a great
while essaying to get in, and at last she went
away, and he returned safe home, his servants
having been much perplexed for him, and having walked about and shot off pieces and hal-
looed in the night, but he heard them not."

IV.

The ship "Lyon" came again in the following
November, bringing from England Governor
Winthrop's wife and the rest of the family, as
well as John Eliot, and many others. Every
ship brought more people: Boston grew.

Life in such a new country could give the
colonists little leisure; artisans of all kinds
were in great demand. Builders, masons, car-
penters, stone-cutters, joiners, cobblers, had
more than they could do. Men who were not
skilled in any such craft became hewers of wood
and drawers of water, or busied themselves with
hunting, fishing, digging, planting, reaping, to
keep the colony from starving. Upon the
women fell the care of the households, and the
spinning, weaving, and fashioning of garments.
Governor Winthrop himself, for example's sake
and because he wished to bear his share of
the labor, worked heartily with his own hands
whenever he saw need.

A great happiness and hope carried the Puritans through the trials of these first hard years. The freedom which they had come so far to seek was found. They now ordered their lives as they thought God willed that they should order them, and in this they were not hindered by any man. Looking forward to the future, they could see that their children and their children's children might do the same.

Though they were still subjects of King Charles, they were more loyal to their church than to any king. They cared more for its welfare than for England. The church ruled the town. Its meetings called together old and young. The first meeting-house stood on King Street, — State Street, now; Brazier's Building covers its site. Three times on Sunday, and several times through the week besides, the people gathered to listen to their minister, their church "teacher," their elders, or their deacons. Church was rest and healing to the weary in spirit, courage and fresh strength to the strong.

No time had these earnest folk for trifling.
A dance was held to be a sinful waste of hours;
theatres were left behind, it was hoped, forever.
Yet the boys and girls were not wholly without
play; out-door sports were in favor, and in-door
games by no means despised. Adam Winthrop's days were surely far from dull; his
father wrote: "The governour and some company with him went up by Charles River about
eight miles above Watertown, and named the
first brook on the north side of the river (being
a fair stream, and coming from a pond a mile
from the river) Beaver Brook, because the
beavers had shorn down divers great trees
there, and made divers dams across the brook.
Thence they went to a great rock, upon which
stood a high stone cleft in sunder, that four
men might go through, which they called Adam's Chair, because the youngest of their company was Adam Winthrop." And again, —
"The governour, Mr. Nowell, Mr. Eliot, and
others, went over Mistick River at Medford,
and going N. and by E. among the rocks

about two or three miles, they came to a very great pond, having in the midst an island of about one acre, and very thick with trees of pine and beech; and the pond had divers small rocks, standing up here and there in it, which they therefore called Spot Pond. They went all about it upon the ice. From thence (towards the N. W. about half a mile) they came to the top of a very high rock, beneath which (towards the N.) lies a goodly plain, part open land and part woody, from whence there is a fair prospect; but it being then close and rainy, they could see but a small distance. This place they called Cheese Rock, because, when they went to eat somewhat, they had only cheese (the governour's man forgetting, for haste, to put up some bread.)"

Vanity of dress was frowned down. Young girls might not flaunt gay ribbons, nor must the gowns of their mothers be too rich or fine. Sober tints, quiet manners, were the rule. The Governor went plainly clad.

Late hours were forbidden; at nine o'clock out went the lights. Nine was the curfew hour,

the "*couvre-feu*" time. In the villages of old
England a bell tolled the day to rest. Here
in New England no bell had been heard as yet:
a drum sounded the curfew here, and beat to
church on Sundays. Nightly, when its roll was
heard, embers were raked together and covered
with ashes, that they might live to kindle the
morrow's flame. Flint and tinder-box were at
hand, to be used in case the coals should die;
but with proper care the coals did not die, and
a glow was ready each morning to warm the
stiffened fingers that searched for its welcome
heat. Our way of flashing fire from a phos-
phorus-tipped wand would have seemed like
magic to Governor Winthrop's boys.

A watch walked the streets throughout the
night, shouting the hour with an " All 's well!"
Lamps for the street or light-houses for the
shore there were none. Darkness settled over
land and sea when the sun was gone.

Wood was always a great lack in Boston.
In 1637 Governor Winthrop wrote to his son,

"We at Boston were almost ready to brake up for want of wood." The hill-sides did not bear enough to supply the towns-people with fuel; logs had to be brought from the mainland or the islands.

Governor Winthrop's own wood-pile was never low, for he had forest-trees upon his farm on the Mystic; but some of his poorer neighbors were in sore need. This is what he did for one of them: ". . . In an hard and long winter, when wood was very scarce at Boston, a man gave him [Governor Winthrop] a private information that a needy person in the neighborhood stole wood sometimes from his pile; whereupon the governour in a seeming anger did reply, 'Does he so? I 'll take a course with him; go, call that man to me; I 'll warrant you I 'll cure him of stealing.' When the man came, the governour, considering that if he had stolen, it was more out of necessity than disposition, said unto him, 'Friend, it is a severe winter, and I doubt you are but meanly provided for wood; wherefore I would have you supply yourself at my wood-pile till this cold season be over.' And then he merrily asked his friends ' Whether he had not effectually cured this man of stealing his wood?'"[1]

Years came and went. Boston prospered. Twelve times was John Winthrop chosen governor of the colony. In 1649 he died. The good he did lives still.

Listen again to Mather's praise of him: " Yea, the governour sometimes made his own *private purse* to be the publick ; not by *sucking* into it, but by *squeezing* out of it." " 'T was his custom also to send some of his family upon errands unto the houses of the poor, about their *meal time*, on purpose to spy whether they *wanted;* and if it were found that they wanted, he would make *that* the opportunity of sending supplies unto them."

He was " The *terror* of the wicked, and the *delight* of the sober, the *envy* of the many, but the *hope* of those who had any hopeful design in hand for the common good of the nation. . . ."

[1] Cotton Mather, Magnalia.

NOTES.

NOTES.

SEPARATISTS AND PURITANS IN ENGLAND.

PAGE 1.

James's reign, 1603–1625.

For James's sayings, and his dealings with the Non-conformists, see Palfrey's *History of New England,* I., Chap. III.; also Green's *History of the English People,* Vol. III., Chap. III.

PAGE 2.

The name Puritan seems to have been given first to the followers of Novatus, a presbyter of the church of Rome. They were called *Cathari,* or, the Pure, and were distinguished by their extreme rigor toward the "lapsed." In later times the same name was applied, as a term of reproach, to the Non-conformists. Fuller, quoted in Young, says that those who refused to subscribe to the liturgy, ceremonies, and discipline of the church were "branded with the odious name of *Puritans*"; accepting the name, the Non-conformists put their own meaning into it. Fuller adds, that some of them were "so far from opposing the liturgy that they endeavored . . . to accompany the minister with a *pure* heart, and labored . . . for a life *pure* and holy." An old English writer of the church of England says : " They are called Puritans who would have the church thoroughly reformed; that is, purged from all those inventions which have been brought into it since the age of the Apostles; and reduced entirely to the Scripture *purity*." [Taken from notes in Young, p. 13.]

Bradford, in Young's *Chronicles of the Pilgrims*, p. 442, speaks of a church formed in Elizabeth's reign, and one before that in Queen Mary's time. Read also Hunter's *Founders of New Plymouth*, and E. D. Mead's "*Why did the Pilgrim Fathers come to New England?*" in Vol. XLI. of the *New Englander*.

PAGES 5, 6.

For Charles's reign (1625–1649) **and the civil war**, see Green's *History of the English People*, Vol. III., Book VII.

THE POKANOKET AND MASSACHUSETTS INDIANS.

PAGE 7.

Columbus, discovering San Salvador in 1492, thought he had approached the eastern shore of India, and therefore called the natives Indians. Though he afterward touched the shores of both Americas, he never knew that he had reached two great new continents. [Read Chap. V. of Higginson's *Young Folks' History of the United States*.]

"**I have seen half a hundred of their wigwams.**" [Josselyn's *Voyages*.]

PAGE 8.

"**Their houses,**" etc. [*Historical Collections of the Indians in New England*, Gookin. p. 9.]

PAGE 12.

Bents. Stalks of coarse grass.

PAGE 13.

Wilk. Whelk.
Targets. Targes or shields.

PAGE 14.

" **The manner of their action,**" etc. [Wood's *New England's Prospect*, Part II., Chap. XII.]

PAGE 15.

Indian tribes. [Read Drake's *Book of the Indians;* Gookin's *Historical Collections of the Indians in New England;* Palfrey's *History of New England*, Vol. I., Chap. III.; and Chap. III. of Higginson's *History.*]

The Indians of Massachusetts Bay. Little is known of the early history of the Indians living in the neighborhood of " the great bay of the Massachusetts." Hutchinson says, — Vol. I., p. 460, of his *History of Massachusetts Bay,* — that the Massachusetts sachem had his seat upon a small hill in the midst of a body of salt marsh in the township of Dorchester, near Squantum.

Nonantum was the old name of Newton; Punkapoag of Stoughton.

PAGE 16.

The Pokanokets. Pokanoket was a general name for the northern shore of Narragansett Bay, including Swansea and Bristol; and the name extended itself to the Indians of that region, and clans closely allied to them.

Massasoit had a wigwam at Sowams, now Warren, R.I.,

and probably another at Mount Hope. [See Fessenden's *History of Warren, R.I.*, published with Tustin's *Historical Discourse*. Also Davis's *Ancient Landmarks of Plymouth*, p. 37.]

For mention of the Pokanoket chieftains, see Young's *Chronicles of the Pilgrims*. Corbitant lived at Gardner's Neck.

Smith. [Read *Adventures and Discoveries of Captain John Smith*, edited by John Ashton and published by Cassell & Co.]

PAGES 17, 18.

Hunt. [See Palfrey's *History of New England*, I., 94. Also Smith's *Description of New England*, 65, 66; and Vol. II., Book VI., p. 176 of his *Generall Historie of Virginia, New England, and the Summer Iles.*]

Maligo. Malaga.

"Rials of eight" (*rial*, from royal). A rial was a gold coin formerly current in England. A rial of eight was worth eight shillings sterling.

Squanto. [See *Bradford*, p. 94.] Some authors speak of Waymouth as Squanto's kidnapper. Hunt was probably the man. [See Drake's *Book of the Indians*, Book II., Chap. II.; also Dermer's letter in Purchas's *Pilgrims*, Vol. IV., p. 1778.]

Mr. John Slainie was interested in a plantation in Newfoundland, and probably sent Squanto thither. Dermer knew that Squanto, who was with Captain Mason, might be useful in making peace with the Cape Cod or Pokanoket Indians whom Hunt had wronged, and for that reason arranged to keep him. Before exploring the coast, Dermer had to go

back to England, and probably took Squanto with him.
Returning in 1619, he sailed with him to Cape Cod.
[Dermer's Letter.]

The Plague. [See Drake, and Dermer's Letter.] Dermer
says : " I passed along the coast where I found some ancient
plantations [Indian villages] not long since populous, now
utterly void ; in other places a remnant remains, but not free
of sickness. Their disease the plague, for we might per-
ceive the sores of some that had escaped. . . ." At Namasket
Dermer was visited by " two kings," Massasoit and Quadequina. At Namasket, too, Squanto saved his master's life.
The savages planned to kill Dermer, but Squanto's entreaties
moved them, and Dermer was spared. After leaving Cape
Cod, Dermer went back to Monhegan, touching at " Masta-
chusit " [Massachusetts] by the way. From Monhegan
he set out upon another southward voyage, this time
without Squanto, and says: " We had not now that faire
quarter amongst the savages as before, which, I take it, was
by reason of our savage's [Squanto's] absence, who desired
(in regard of our long journey) to stay with some of our
savage friends at Sawahquatooke. . . ."

Soon after this, Squanto regained his freedom wholly, for
Dermer while in Virginia was seized with a fever and died.
Squanto returned to Namasket.

Destruction of the Massachusetts clans. [See Drake,
Book II.. Chap. II., 16.] Drake quotes Morton's *New
English Canaan:* " As I travelled in that forest near the
Massachusetts, it seemed to me a new-found Golgotha."
[See also Book II., Chap. III.] The Tarratines, who lived
further to the north, were the enemies of the Massachusetts.

THE PILGRIMS. — I. THE FLIGHT FROM ENGLAND.

PAGES 20, 21.

"**The manor house of Scrooby**, built originally as a hunting-seat for the archbishops of York, though in Brewster's time 'much decayed,' had been occupied for many years by his father as bailiff for the archbishop." [*Winsor's Narrative and Critical History of America*, 259.]

The cut, "Site of the Manor House," taken, by permission, from the above, represents the scene as it was thirty years ago. The manor house has "long since passed away." [Mr. Deane, in *Mass. Hist. Soc. Proc.*, XI., 404.]

"The sycamores themselves, one of which is shown in the view, . . . are supposed . . . to mark the site of the main building, now destroyed and gone." [Henry M. Dexter, in Vol. I. of *Sabbath at Home*, p. 137.]

William Brewster was born about 1564. He had obtained a good education, and "served that religious and godly gentleman, Mr. Davison, during years when he was Secretary of State." [Young, 463.] Mr. Davison was a Puritan. After leaving Mr. Davison, Brewster held the office of postmaster at Scrooby. His name is found in the postmaster-general's account: "William Brewster, Post of Scrooby, for his wages at 2s. per diem, for 183 days, . . . ended the last of Sept., 1607, £18. 6s." [*The Founders of New Plymouth*, Hunter, p. 67.]

William Bradford, b. March 19, 1589–90 ; d. May 9, 1657. [See Mr. Charles Deane's preface to Bradford's *History of Plymouth Plantation*, Mass. Hist. Coll., Vol. III., Fourth Series. Also Rev. Joseph Hunter's *Founders of New Plymouth*.]

Bradford's parents died when he was very young. He was a delicate, studious boy, poring over his books oftener than joining out-door sports, and thoughtful beyond his years. His uncles were well-to-do farmers, and were among the chief families of Austerfield. Austerfield is described by Palfrey, Vol. I., p. 134, as at present "a hamlet of perhaps thirty brick houses, roofed with tiles. At least two of them look as if they had been standing in Bradford's time."

PAGES 23, 24, 25.

James I. and Puritanism in England. [See Palfrey, Vol. I., Chap. III.]

"Some were taken," etc. [Bradford.]

Flight to Holland, 1607–8 [Hunter, 89]. "Under color of a royal proclamation which had been obtained by Bancroft, forbidding the king's subjects to transport themselves to Virginia without his special license, or under some other pretence, the embarkation of the Scrooby people was obstructed" [Palfrey, Vol. I., 138]. The account of the attempts is taken from Bradford.

II. THE VOYAGE TO AMERICA.

PAGE 26.

See Bradford's *History of Plymouth Plantation*, in Mass. Hist. Coll., Vol. III., Fourth Series.

"After . . . some 11 or 12 years (which is ye more observable being ye whole time of y^t famous truce between that State and the Spaniards) . . . they began to incline to this conclusion, of remoovall to some other place. . . . They

saw that . . . within a few years more they would be in danger to scatter, . . . or sink under their burdens, or both. . . .
But that which was . . . of all sorowes most heavie to be
borne, was that many of their children . . . were drawne
away by evill examples . . . getting y⁰ raines off their neks
and departing from their parents. Some became souldiers,
others took upon them far viages by sea and other some,
worse courses. . . ." [From the above, pp. 22–24.]

While in Leyden, Bradford earned a scant living by working at the manufacture of silk. Brewster taught, and also
had some success as a printer. [See Young's *Chronicles*,
and Dexter's *Mourt's Relation*.]

PAGE 27.

Grant of land and James's connivance. [See Palfrey,
I., 151.] Cushman, Carver, and Brewster helped arrange
matters in England.

Edward Winslow, b. 1594, d. 1655, was "a gentleman of
the best family of any of the Plymouth planters. . . . He was
not one of the original band of Pilgrims who escaped to Holland in 1608, but, being on his travels, fell in with them
at Leyden, in 1617." [Hutchinson, quoted in Young's
Chronicles of the Pilgrims, p. 274.]

William Brewster, the elder of the church, was to act as
pastor in America. The Pilgrims hoped that Mr. Robinson
would join them, but Mr. Robinson died in Holland, and
Mr. Brewster preached in Plymouth for a number of years.
Brewster's sons, Love and Wrestling, sailed with him in the
Mayflower; his daughters, Patience and Fear, came later
with their mother.

John Carver was one of the deacons of the church at Leyden, and was to be the governor of the colony. [Young, 200.]

Myles Standish was born in Lancashire, England. He is believed to be descended from Ralph Standish and Thurston de Standish. Two branches of the family lived in England: these were the Standishes of Standish, and the Standishes of Duxbury Hall. Standish is about eighteen miles north-east from Liverpool, Duxbury a few miles northeast from Standish. For the genealogy of the Standishes of Duxbury Hall, see Burke's *History of the Commoners*, Vol. IV., p. 642. Myles probably belonged to the Duxbury branch. His will shows that he considered himself heir to estates wrongfully withheld from him.

He went to Holland as lieutenant in one of the regiments sent to aid the Dutch in their war with Spain. The twelve years of peace left him without employment; he became a friend of the English at Leyden, and joined their company when they emigrated to America. He was not originally a member of their church, but joined them from personal good-will or a liking for the adventure. [See Young, 125.]

He died in 1656.

We think of him, always and rightly, as Longfellow describes him : —

" Short of stature he was, but strongly built and athletic,
   Broad in the shoulders, deep-chested, with muscles and sinews
      of iron;
   Brown as a nut was his face, but his russet beard was already
   Flaked with patches of snow, as hedges sometimes in November."

And again : —

"Though he was rough, he was kindly; she knew how during the
  winter
He had attended the sick, with a hand as gentle as woman's;
Somewhat hasty and hot, he could not deny it, and headstrong,
Stern, as a soldier might be, but hearty, and placable always,
Not to be laughed at and scorned, because he was little of stature;
For he was great of heart, magnanimous, courtly, courageous."

[*Courtship of Miles Standish.*]

PAGE 28.

Agreement with the Merchant Adventurers. The Pilgrims were too poor to fit out their expedition themselves.
Mr. Thomas Weston and others, known as the "Merchant
Adventurers," furnished money for the undertaking; and
upon hard terms. All the gain of the colony was to be kept
strict account of during seven years; at the end of that time
it was to be divided among the colonists and the adventurers; each man receiving more or less, according to the
amount of money or labor expended by him. An adventurer
lending ten pounds would receive as much at the end of the
seven years as a colonist who had had no money to con-
tribute, but who had given all those years of steady labor.
Ten pounds was accounted a single share, and each person's seven years of work was rated at that amount. [See
Davis's *Ancient Landmarks of Plymouth*, Part I., p. 15.]

"The Dutch offered to transport them freely, and furnish
every family with cattle if they would 'go under them to
Hudson's River,' and become citizens of New Netherlands.
Instead of accepting this offer, as at one time they were
almost on the point of doing, they finally made bond-

servants of themselves to the Merchant Adventurers for
seven years . . . for the sake of planting themselves in New
England." [E. D. Mead's "*Why did the Pilgrim Fathers
come to New England?*" *New Englander*, Vol. XLI., p. 720.]

Departure from Delftshaven. [Palfrey, 156; Bradford,
58, 59; Young, 384.]

The Speedwell. A small vessel of about sixty tons.
[Young.] The master of the Speedwell was afterward
thought to have exaggerated the state of the vessel, in order
that he might slip out of his contract and escape the dangerous voyage. [Young, 98; Bradford, 70.]

PAGE 29.

The Mayflower was a vessel of "nine score" tons. [Brad-
ford, 58.] The list of her passengers, 102 in all, may be
found in Bradford, 447. Those who went back after the
final "sifting" were such as were least able to bear hardship
or were not unwilling to return. [Bradford, 70–72.]

PAGE 30.

"**They gott into the cape harbor**" (Nov. 11, 1620).
[Bradford, 77.] Their grant gave them permission to settle
near Hudson's River; they had not permission to occupy
Plymouth or any part of the Cape Cod region.

III. DISCOVERIES.

PAGES 30–36.

"**The Mayflower anchored** within half a furlong of the
end of Long Point, two miles from the present village
of Provincetown." [Young, 120.] For the account of

Standish's first exploring party, which set out Wednesday, Nov. 15, see Young, 127–137. The maps of Cape Cod and Plymouth are from Dexter's edition of *Mourt's Relation.*

The formal compact. Signed Nov. 11, before the ship came to anchor. [Young, 120.]

PAGE 37.

The second search. About thirty-four men set off in the shallop. They sailed to Pamet River, landed at Indian Neck, marched several miles by the side of the river, or creek, and then, wet as they were through previous wading, slept through the night under some pine trees in the snow. The next morning they went again to Hopkins's cliff, which they now named Cornhill, and with their "curtlaxes" (cutlasses) and swords hewed and carved the frozen, snowy ground till they came to more of the corn stored there, getting some ten bushels in all. Some of the party had already fallen ill from exposure. These were now sent to the ship by the shallop, which was to go and return to the explorers with all speed. While waiting for it to return, they marched into the woods, finding a grave and the bones of a man and a child. [Young, 138–146.]

"**The houses,**" etc. [Young, 144.]

Trunches. Short stakes.

IV. THE FIRST ENCOUNTER.

PAGES 38, 39.

The last search. This party, eighteen in all, sailed past the shore of Truro toward Billingsgate Point. They saw some Indians on the shore near Eastham. Landing a

league or two south of them, the explorers camped for the
night. In the morning they found that the Indians had
been busy cutting up a grampus. After this they saw an
Indian burying-ground surrounded by a palisade ; they
also came upon some more houses and two baskets of
parched acorns, but no people. Their rendezvous for that
night, when the Nausets alarmed them, was probably at
Great Meadow Creek. The account given on pp. 38-45 is
from Young, 150-162.

PAGE 40.

Captain Hunt, etc. [See Bradford, 95, and p. 17 of this
volume.]

PAGE 42.

After leaving "The First Encounter," the shallop sailed
toward Plymouth. A snow-storm which soon came on
"prevented their seeing Sandy Neck, and led them to over-
shoot Barnstable Harbor. Had it not been for this, it is
highly probable that they would have entered and made
their settlement there." [Young, 159, note.]

For further accounts of the night and day spent beside
and on Clark's Island, and the landing at Plymouth, see
Young, 160-162, and Bradford, 87.

The rock, which was probably then and later used as a
landing-place, is to be seen at Plymouth.

Some men who went ashore on the day of arrival brought
back to the ship a boat-load of juniper, or red cedar, "which
smelled very sweet and strong, and of which we burnt the
most part of the time we lay there." Juniper, sassafras, and
birch are mentioned as having been found at that time.

While Bradford was away upon the final search, his wife

Dorothy fell overboard and was drowned. [Mather's *Magnalia*, Vol. I., Book II., p. 103.]

Peregrine White was born while the Mayflower lay near Provincetown. [Davis's *Ancient Landmarks of Plymouth*, Part II., 283.]

V. PLYMOUTH.

PAGE 45.

Charles I., when only Prince Charles, a boy of sixteen, looked over Captain Smith's map, and gave English names to many points on the New England coast. Only three of his names have held their original places on our shore. They are Plymouth; Cape Ann, named for his mother, Anne of Denmark; and the River Charles. See Smith's *Generall Historie*, Book VI., p. 76, for a list of the names given by Charles.

PAGE 46.

The Christmas record. [Young, 169.]

Their fathers were proud, etc. Palfrey calls their feeling one of " stern exultation." [Vol. I., p. 173.]

PAGES 47, 48, 49.

The houses were built of hewn logs, with mortar made of mud and sand; and covered on top by beams and rafters on which was fastened a thatching of reeds and boughs. This thatching was very apt to catch fire from sparks flying out of the chimneys. A building in which William Bradford and Governor Carver lay ill, caught thus, and the sick men were forced to make a speedy escape. [Young, 177.]

For a plan showing the seven houses, see Davis, Part I., p. 53.

Bradford had suffered severely from exposure to wet and cold in the voyages of discovery. [Young, 174.]
" **Mr. Edward Winslow**, his wife," etc. [Bradford, 447.]
" **Scarce fifty remained.**" [Bradford, 91.]
Mr. Robinson's letter may be found in Young, 473.
Levelling the graves. [*Ancient Landmarks of Plymouth*, Davis, Part I., p. 129.]

VI. SAMOSET, SQUANTO, AND MASSASOIT.

PAGES 50, 51.

See Young, 180–196 ; Bradford, 93–95. Also " *The Pokanoket Indians*" in this volume.
Monhegan. An island off the coast of Maine.
" **He very boldly.**" [Young, 182.]
With " five other tall proper men." [Same, p. 186.]

PAGE 52.

Massasoit. [See E. W. Pierce's *Indian History*.]

PAGE 55.

" **A greene rugge**," etc. [Young, 193.]
Massasoit " marvelled much," etc. [Same, 195.]
" **A very lusty man,**" etc. [Same.]

VII. THE FIRST SUMMER.

PAGE 56.

Alden had been hired at Southampton as a cooper. He came upon the understanding that he might return to England or remain in America, as he should see fit. He stayed,

and in 1621 married Priscilla Mullins. Tradition says that
Standish wished to marry Priscilla, and that she answered
his messenger, Alden, with, " Why don't you speak for yourself, John? "

The first marriage in Plymouth, however, was not John
Alden's, but Edward Winslow's. Winslow's first wife and
Mrs. White's husband died, the former March 24, the latter
Feb. 21, 1621 ; and the survivors of the two broken mar-
riages, with a despatch probably due to the practical needs
of the time, were united in May. The ceremony, " according to yᵉ custome of yᵉ Low Countries in which they had
lived, was . . . performed by the magistrate," not by the
minister. " And this practice hath continued in these parts
to this time. Anⁿ 1646." [Bradford, 101.]

Carver's death (April, 1621). "*Whilst*," etc. [Bradford,
100.]

The journey to Pokanoket (June or July, 1621). "*Having
in some sort*," etc. The quoted passages on pp. 59, 60 are
from Young, pp. 202–213. See Bradford, 102, and consult
the map at the beginning of this volume.

Journey to Nauset (latter part of July, or early in August
1621). The quotations on pp. 62–64 are from Young, 214–
218. Billington, the father of the boy, was a wretched sort of
man, executed in 1630 for murder. Francis Billington, the
boy's brother, climbing one day to the top of a tree on a hill
not far from Plymouth, saw a large double pond, which he
thought was a sea. It has since been called Billington's Sea.

Hobamok. This friendly Indian attached himself to the captain as Squanto did to the governor. [See Bradford, 103 and 114.]

Attack on Corbitant's wigwam (Aug. 14, 1621). [Young, 220–223.]

PAGES 65, 66.

They had much firmer peace. [Bradford, 104.] Chickataubot signed the treaty of peace, as did Corbitant and Canacum. [Young, Note, 232.]

The journey to Massachusetts. [See *The Memorial History of Boston*, Vol. I., Chap. III., and Young's *Chronicles of the Pilgrims*, 224–229.]

" On the afternoon of Wednesday, the 29th of September, 1621, a large open sail-boat, or shallop, as it was then called, entered Boston Harbor, coming up along the shore from the direction of Plymouth. In it were thirteen men, — ten Europeans, with three savages acting as their guides. The whole party was under the immediate command of Captain Miles Standish, and their purpose was to explore the country in and about Massachusetts Bay, as Boston Harbor was then called. . . . Passing by Point Allerton, they laid their course for what appeared to them to be the bottom of the bay, and, finding good shelter there, came to anchor off what is now known as Thomson's Island. Here they lay during the night, which they passed on board their boat. . . .

" Early the next morning the party made ready to extend their explorations to the mainland. As they had come to establish relations with what remained of the once powerful tribe of the Massachusetts, their Indian guides seem to have

brought them to that point . . . which was most convenient
for access to the broad plain . . . known as the ' Massachusetts Fields,' from its being used as the central gathering-
place of the tribe. This plain lay in the northern part of
what is now the town of Quincy, and . . . was connected
with the Squantum headland . . . by a low neck of marsh
and beach. . . . Standish landed at the foot of the bold
rocky cliff [Squaw Rock, or Squantum Head]."

Here they met a woman who told them where to find her
sachem, Obbatinewat; and they sailed to a point probably
near Savin Hill or Dorchester Heights, his tarrying-place.
"Obbatinewat then undertook to guide the party to the
Squaw Sachem, who lived somewhere on the Mystic, in the
neighborhood, it is supposed, of Wachuset." The Squaw
Sachem was the widow of Nanepashmet, a Massachusetts
chief who had been killed by the Tarratines. The party did
not reach her home; they landed and explored the country
in the neighborhood of Medford and Winchester, found
Nanepashmet's deserted wigwam and a palisade enclosure
within which he was buried, and bought a few skins from
some Indian women, but were obliged to return without
having made a treaty with any save Obbatinewat, who was
but a starveling chief, tributary to Massasoit, and equally
afraid of the Squaw Sachem and of the Tarratines. [From
Memorial History, I., Chap. III.]

Young, in a note, p. 226, suggests that Squantum "may
have been so called by them at this time for their interpreter, Tisquantum, who was of the party."

VIII. Feasting and Famine.

Pages 66-69.

Harvest. [*Chronicles of Pilgrims*, 231.]
Thanksgiving. [Same.]

Page 70.

Thirty-five new settlers came in the Fortune. [See Bradford, 105; *Chronicles of the Pilgrims*, 234; *New England Chronology*, 198.] A charter, granting them legal right to the land upon which they were already seated, — land which was not within the limits of the patent under which they came, — was probably brought over in this ship. It may be seen at Plymouth. [Note in Bradford, 107.]

"**Ye great people of ye Narrogansetts,**" etc. [See Bradford, 110.] This occurred in December, 1621. Longfellow represents Standish as cramming the snake-skin with bullets, and, for the sake of the dramatic action and situation, places the episode before the sailing of the Mayflower, whereas the vessel had already returned the preceding April. The poem also seizes upon Standish's combat with Pecksuot, which really occurred in 1623, and brings it into the same range of time.

Page 71.

The snake-skin returned. [See Young's *Chronicles of the Pilgrims*, 284.]

They agreed to inclose their dwellings. [Bradford, 111.]

Governor Bradford closes his account of the year 1621 as follows: "And herewith I shall end this year. Only I shall remember one passage more, rather of mirth than of weight. On ye day called Christmas-day, ye Govr called them out to worke, (as was used,) but ye most of this new company [those who had come in the Fortune,] excused themselves and said it went against their consciences to work on y^t day. So ye Govr tould them that if they made it a matter of conscience he would spare them till they were better informed. So he led away ye rest and left them ; but when they came home at noone from their worke, he found them in ye streete at play, openly; some pitching ye barr and some at stooleball [a game in which a ball is driven from stool to stool] and such like sports. So he went to them, and tooke away their implements, and tould them that was against his conscience, that they should play and others worke. If they made ye keeping of it matter of devotion, let them keep their houses, but there should be no gaming or revelling in ye streets. Since which time nothing has been attempted in that way, at least openly." [p. 112.]

PAGES 72, 73.

Mr. Weston's men. [Young, 296.] They came in the Charity and the Swan, arriving in July, 1622.

Much was stolen. [Bradford, 126.]

The fort. [Same.]

" **A large square house,**" and "**they assembled by beat of drum.**" [De Rasiere.]

Tisquantum's death (November, 1622). [Bradford, 128.]

PAGE 74.

Standish at Manomet (March, 1623). [Young, 309-312.]

"In came two of the Massachusetts men," etc. [Young, 309-312.]

IX. MASSASOIT'S ILLNESS.

PAGES 76-82.

The account is taken from Winslow, in Young, 313.

X. VICTORY.

PAGE 83.

Massasoit's warning was seconded by news brought by one of the Wessagusset settlers, who came to Plymouth "with a small pack on his back," pursued by the Indians, and only saved from them by fortunately losing his way and wandering out of the direct path along which they were following him. "He apprehended they . . . would be all knokt in ye head shortly." Then says Bradford, "This made them make ye more hast, and dispatched a boat away wth Captain Standish. . . ." [Bradford, 132. See also Young, 332-336.]

Standish at Wessagusset (March, 1623). [Young, 336.]

PAGES 84, 85, 86.

"So base were they," etc. [Bradford, p. 130.]

Encounter with Pecksuot and Wituwamat. [Young, 337-339.] Longfellow says : —

"Then stood Pecksuot forth, self-vaunting, insulting Miles Standish;
While with his fingers he patted the knife that hung at his bosom,
Drawing it half from its sheath, and plunging it back, as he muttered.
'By and by it shall see; it shall eat; ah, ha! but shall speak not!
This is the mighty captain the white men have sent to destroy us!
He is a little man; let him go and work with the women!'"

And of Standish : —

" All the hot blood of his race, of Sir Hugh and of Thurston de
    Standish,
  Boiled and beat in his heart, and swelled in the veins of his temples.
  Headlong he leaped on the boaster, and, snatching his knife from its
    scabbard,
  Plunged it into his heart, and, reeling backward, the savage
  Fell with his face to the sky, and a fiendlike fierceness upon it."

Then, —

" Silent, with folded arms stood Hobomok, friend of the white man.
  Smiling at length he exclaimed to the stalwart captain of Plymouth,
  'Pecksuot bragged very loud of his courage, his strength, and his
    stature, —
  Mocked the great captain and called him a little man; but I see now
  Big enough have you been to lay him speechless before you.'
  Thus the first battle was fought and won by the stalwart Miles
    Standish.
  When the tidings thereof were brought to the village of Plymouth,
  And as a trophy of war the head of the brave Wattawamat
  Scowled from the roof of the fort, which at once was a church and a
    fortress,
  All who beheld it rejoiced, and praised the Lord and took courage.
  Only Priscilla averted her face from this spectre of terror,
  Thanking God in her heart that she had not married Miles Standish;
  Shrinking, fearing almost, lest, coming home from his battles,
  He should lay claim to her hand, as the prize and reward of his
    valor."

Wituwamat's head was, indeed, set up upon the fort, but
Priscilla had then been married two years. The poem alters
dates at need.

PAGE 87.

Death of Canacum, etc.   [Young, 345.]

The Indian's season for planting corn is "when the leaves of the white oak are as big as a mouse's ear." [Note in Young, 230.]

PAGES 88, 89.

Bradford has little regard for those who hold that private wealth should be done away with, and land and goods become common property. "As if they were wiser than God!" [p. 135.]

Drought and day of fasting and prayer (July, 1623). [*Chronicles of Pilgrims*, p. 349.]

PAGES 90, 91.

Arrival of the Anne and Little James. [Bradford, pp. 142–147.] Bradford and Mrs. Southworth had known each other in England, and a correspondence between them led to her coming over to be married to him.

The Third Harvest (about the middle of September, 1623). [Bradford, 147.]

ADDITIONAL NOTES ON THE PILGRIMS.

Three heifers and a bull were brought over in 1624 in the Charity. [Davis's *Ancient Landmarks of Plymouth*.] These were the first cattle that had come to New England. Priscilla may have had many a ride upon the back of a white steer, but on her wedding-day she can have proceeded only in such state as could be furnished by her own two feet.

"**From 1621 to 1657**, the year of his death, Bradford was annually chosen governor, with the exception of 1633-

1636, and 1644, when Edward Winslow was chosen, and 1634 and 1638, when Thomas Prince was chosen. . . . It is probable that in the excepted years he was dropped at his own request." [Davis's *Ancient Landmarks of Plymouth*.]

In **1627** the Pilgrims made a new arrangement with the Adventurers. "The terms of this compact were that for eighteen hundred pounds, to be paid at the Royal Exchange every Michaelmas, in nine equal annual instalments, the first in 1628, the company sold to them [the Pilgrims] all their interest in the plantation, including merchandise and lands. . . . Several of the chief planters entered into bonds for the fulfilment of the contract." [Barry's *Hist. of Mass.*, I., 139.]

"The debt of eighteen hundred pounds to the Adventurers, and a debt to other parties amounting to six hundred more, were assumed by William Bradford, Miles Standish, Isaac Allerton, Edward Winslow, William Brewster, John Howland, and Thomas Prince," to whom were joined four friends in London. [Davis, 57.]

These men paid off the debts within the time prescribed, by entering into a brisk trade for fur, etc., with the natives. Some of the Indians used bits of shell, which they called wampum, for money. The Pilgrims taught other tribes to use it, and it became the common currency. "No legal tender scheme, in these later days, has been bolder in its conception or more successful in its career than that of the Pilgrim Fathers, which, with the shells of the shore, relieved their community from debt, and established on a permanent basis the wealth and prosperity of New England. . . . This currency of the early days was made from the purple and

white parts of the quaw-haug shell, round, about a sixteenth
of an inch in thickness, and a quarter of an inch in diam-
eter, with a hole in the middle for stringing on strings of
bark or hemp, the purple and white alternating on the string,
the purple of double the value of the white, and the whole
valued at five shillings per fathom.   Strings of this wampum
may be seen in Pilgrim Hall, in Plymouth, which have been
preserved in the . . . families of the old colony, and used as
necklaces and other ornaments after their use as currency
had become obsolete."   [Davis, 58. See also Bradford,
212–214.]

In 1631 Standish, Brewster, Alden, and some others,
finding Plymouth crowded, and wishing more room for their
farms than they could conveniently get within its limits,
removed to Duxbury.   Standish settled on Captain's Hill,
Brewster near him, Alden rather further away.   Some de-
scendants of Governor Bradford, when asked "Why did not
John Alden live nearer his friend?" replied, "Oh, perhaps
both sides thought it as well that they should have a little
distance between them."   But the distance was not so great
as to prevent Standish's son Alexander from falling in love
with Priscilla's daughter, Sarah; their marriage is recorded
in Davis's *Ancient Landmarks of Plymouth*, Part II., p. 250.

Two troublesome members of the colony, Oldham, who
came in the Anne, and Lyford, who arrived later, were ban-
ished from Plymouth and went to Hull, or Natascot, as it
was then called.   Mr. Roger Conant, "a pious, sober, and
prudent gentleman," joined them there, as did some others
who disliked the "rigid principles" of the Plymouth rule.
[Prince, *New England Chronology*, 231.]

Conant, Lyford, and Oldham afterward removed from Natascot to Naumkeag, or Salem. [See Palfrey, Vol. I., Chap.
VIII., and Higginson's *Young Folks' Hist.*, Chap. VIII.]

In 1625 another settlement was attempted by a Captain
Wollaston, who brought men to Quincy. A roistering fellow
named Thomas Morton obtained control of this settlement,
which he called Merry Mount. Morton behaved so badly
in selling firearms to the Indians, and in other dealings with
the natives, that Captain Standish was sent to arrest him.
He was captured and sent back to England, but returned
and lived for some time longer at Merry Mount, "escaping
a second arrest only by concealing himself in the woods."
[*Memorial History of Boston*, I., 81.]

BOSTON IN ENGLAND.

PAGE 92.

Botolph and Adulph were of German descent. [See
*Collections for a Topographical and Historical Account of
Boston,* Thompson, p. 223.]

The Engles. [See Green's *History of the English People*,
Vol. I., Chap. I.]

PAGE 95.

Bot-holp, boat-help. [See Jean Ingelow's notes on her
High Tide on the Coast of Lincolnshire, Illustrated Edition.] The "stolen tide" which she writes about is spoken
of in the history of the town : the "Boston bells" are the
bells of old Boston ; the Lindis is the river Witham.

Monastery destroyed by the Danes about 870. [Thomp-
son.]

Name Boston. [Above, and Jean Ingelow.]

St. Botolph's church. "The church . . . is 100 feet wide and 300 feet long within the walls. . . . The tower is the highest (100 yards) and noblest in Europe. It is easily seen 40 miles round this level country, and further by sea. . . . There was a prodigious clock-bell which could be heard 6 or 7 miles round, with many old verses round it. . . . Oliver Cromwell, then a colonel, lay in Boston the night before he fought the battle of Wimeby, near Horncastle, Oct. 10, 1643. [Stukely, quoted by Thompson, p. 57.]

The tower is a lantern tower, built for holding a great light. In former days it served as a beacon. Below the lanterns hung a chime of bells.

The floor of the church was filled with tablets marking the burial-places beneath. Mrs. Hawthorne says that the nave is full of carved oaken seats, and that the pulpits are in the midst of them instead of being in the choir.

Mr. John Cotton. [See Mather's *Life of Cotton*.]

PAGES 96, 97, 98.

Lady Arbella and Mr. Johnson. [See *Memorial History of Boston*, Vol. I., p. 117.]

"A fellow in the town," etc. [Mather, I., 240.]

WILLIAM BLACKSTONE.

The facts concerning William Blackstone are gathered from the *Memorial History of Boston*; Bliss's *History of Rehoboth*; Arnold's *Rhode Island*; Newman's *Address at*

Study Hill; Young's *Chronicles of Massachusetts;* Davis, in
Mass. Hist. Coll. X., 190, 2d series; Hopkins's *History of
Providence*, Mass. Hist. Coll. IX., 2d series; and S. G. Drake's
History of Boston.

I.

PAGES 99–105.

Blackstone, or, as he wrote his name, Blaxton, was about
thirty years old in 1625. [*Memorial History*, Vol. I., p. 84.]

"**He took the freeman's oath** May 18, 1631, being the
first who took it, and before the passing of the order which
restricted the privileges of freemen to church members."
[*History of Rehoboth*, p. 4.]

He received for his land $133.20. [S. C. Newman,
Address at Study Hill.] Each inhabitant of Boston paid at
least sixpence toward the purchase of the land; some paid
more. [Arnold's *History of Rhode Island*, pp. 98, 99.]
His original lot of fifty acres was about one-fifteenth of
Shawmut. [Drake's *History of Boston*, p. 95.]

His stock of cows consisted of two heifers and a bull.
For these he paid $53.28. [Newman's *Address at Study
Hill.*]

II.

PAGES 105–110.

In 1634 he sold his title to all land in Shawmut, except-
ing his six-acre lot; and soon afterward, in 1634 or 1635,
removed to that part of old Rehoboth now known as Lonsdale. [Arnold's *History of Rhode Island*, pp. 98, 99.]

The first horses brought to Boston came in the Mayflower or the Whale, arriving July 1, 1630. [Winthrop's
History of New England, Vol. I., p. 34.]

Anne Pollard's deposition may be read in the Fifth Report of the Record Commissioners.

Mrs. Stevenson lived on Milk Street, on the site afterward occupied by the house in which Franklin was born. [*Memorial History*, p. 84.]

At the time of Blackstone's death, Roger Williams wrote : " About a fortnight since your old acquaintance, Mr. Blackstone, departed this life, in the four-score year of his age." [*Memorial History*. Vol. I., p. 84.]

King Philip's War. Philip was the son of Massasoit. For an account of the war, see Higginson's *History*, Ch. XV.

JOHN WINTHROP.

I.

PAGES 112, 113.

Map of Boston, Old and New.

Shawmut in 1625 was very different in shape from the Boston of to-day. The map on pp. 112, 113 shows the original peninsula [white], surrounded by the new land [shaded]. The Charles River once flowed over what is now the Public Garden, and over mud flats at the west of the Garden, now Commonwealth Avenue, Beacon Street, etc. At especially high tides the water washed over the Neck at Dover Street, and across Hanover or Middle Street, between Mill and Town Coves. For information concerning the growth of the town, see the *Memorial History of Boston*, Vol. I., from which, by kind permission, this map has been reproduced.

PAGE 115.

Puritans. [See references on p. 157.]

PAGE 116.

John Winthrop was born Jan. 22, 1588, in Groton, England, four miles southwest from Hadleigh. His early journals show that he had a strongly religious nature. Indeed, though he became a lawyer, he had at one time serious thoughts of studying for the ministry. His life as a young man was full of sorrow. Married at eighteen, he lost his first wife, and afterward a second; but, with his third marriage, in 1618, to Margaret, daughter of Sir John Tyndal, a period of greater tranquillity began. In 1626 he was appointed one of the practising attorneys of the Court of Wards, a position which he lost or resigned after a few years. "He felt that a crisis was at hand in the condition of England, and . . . was anticipating a personal share in the sufferings to which the friends of civil and religious freedom were about to be subjected." [*Life and Letters of John Winthrop*, Vol. I., 303.] While in this state of uncertainty and anxiety, he was urged by some of his friends to join them in their attempt to found a colony in America. They were going under the auspices of a corporation called the Company of Massachusetts Bay; and he decided to cast his lot with theirs. The following extracts show some of his reasons for doing so : —

"SOME GEN^l CONCLUSIONS . . .

" 1 : It is granted that the worke is lawfull and hopefull of success for the great good of the churche. . . .

"4. The service of sayinge and upholdinge a particular churche is to be preferred before the betteringe some parte of a church alreadye established. . . .

"7: A future good, if it be greater, may be preferred before a present good that is lesse, and in this respecte, the members of that churche may be of more use to their mother churche heere, than manye of those whom she shall still keep in her owne bosome. . . ." [*Life and Letters of John Winthrop*, I., 326.]

PARTICULAR CONSIDERATIONS IN THE CASE OF JOHN WINTHROP.

"1. It is come to that issue as . . . the wellfare of the Plantation depends upon his goeinge, for divers of the Chiefe Undertakers . . . will not goe without him.

"2. He acknowledges a satisfactorye callinge outwarde from those of the Plantation, inwardly by the inclination of his own heart to the work. . . .

"3. Though his means be sufficient for a comfortable subsistence in a private condition heere, yet the one halfe of them being disposed to his 3 elder Sonnes, who are now of age, he cannot live in the same place and callinge with that which remains . . . and so, if he should refuse this opportunity, that talent which God hath bestowed upon him for publike service, were like to be buried.

"4. His wife and suche of his children as are come to years of discretion are voluntarylye disposed to the same course.

"5. Most of his friends . . . do consent to his change." [*Life and Letters*, I., 327.]

He was made governor of the colony.

"And now the Court [a court held by the Massachusetts Bay Company], . . . having received extraordinary great commendations of Mr. John Wynthrop, . . . as one being every (way) well fitted . . . for the place of Governor, — did put in nomination for that place Mr. John Winthrop, Sir R. Saltonstall, Mr. Johnson, and Mr. John Humfry: and the said Mr. Winthrop was . . . chosen to be governor for the ensuing year. . . ." [*Life and Letters*, p. 348. For a full account of the Massachusetts Bay Company, see Palfrey's *History of New England*, Vol. I., Chap. VIII. Read also Higginson's *Young Folks' History of the United States*, Chap. VIII.]

Knowing that there must be no holding back or falling out, he, with the other leaders of the enterprise, signed a paper in which they promised solemnly to be faithful to each other and to their purpose ; ". . . having weighed the greatness of the work in regard of the consequence, God's glory and the church's good . . . it is fully and faithfully *Agreed* amongst us . . . that . . . we will be ready . . . to embark . . . by the first of March next, . . . to the end to pass the seas, (under God's protection,) to inhabit and continue in New England : . . .

(Signed) " Richard Saltenstall,   Thomas Sharpe,
              Thomas Dudley,   Increase Norwell,
              William Vassall,   John Winthrop,
              Nicholas West,   William Pynchon,
              Isaac Johnson,   Kellam Browne,
              John Humfrey,   William Calbron."

[*Life and Letters*, I., 344.]

Lady Arbella was probably the daughter of Thomas, eleventh Baron Clinton, third Earl of Lincoln. [Burke's *Peerage*.] Hawthorne fills out the scant outline which, alone, we have of her life, in his *Grandfather's Chair*.

PAGE 119.

The Arbella, Talbot, Ambrose, and Jewel sailed from Southampton on the 22d of March, 1629–30, and finally from Cowes on April 8. The Arbella was originally named the Eagle, and was a vessel of 350 tons.

Winthrop's Journal. The History of New England was begun at Cowes, Easter Monday, March 22.

The seven other ships were the Charles, the William and Francis, the Hopewell, the Whale, the Success, the Trial, and the Mayflower — the same Mayflower that had carried the Pilgrims to Plymouth ten years before. [*Life and Letters*, Vol. II., p. 4.]

Henry Winthrop sailed in the Talbot ; Adam and Stephen, in the Arbella. [Same, 6.]

PAGE 120.

"Eight vessels," etc. [Winthrop's *History of New England*, Vol. I., p. 7.]

PAGE 122.

The children of the ship. [Same, pp. 10, 11.]

PAGE 124.

Salem. Roger Conant, "a religious, sober, and prudent gentleman" [Hubbard's *History of New England*, Chap. XVIII.], with a few others, settled at Naumkeag, in 1626.

In 1628 John Endicott went from England to Naumkeag to act as manager of the settlement there, in behalf of the Dorchester company, which afterward became merged in the Company of Massachusetts Bay. "The remains of Conant's company were disposed to question the claims of the newcomers. But the dispute was amicably composed, and, in commemoration of its adjustment, the place took the name of 'Salem,' the Hebrew word for *peaceful*." [Palfrey's *History of New England*, Vol. I., Chap. VIII., pp. 285–289. See this chapter, and also Higginson's *Young Folks' History of the United States*, Chap. VIII., for further information concerning Salem.]

Dudley's letter was addressed " to the Right Honourable my very good lady, the Lady Bridget, Countess of Lincoln." [New Hampshire Hist. Coll., Vol. IV., p. 224.] The Lady Bridget was the wife of Theophilus, Lady Arbella's brother.

PAGE 125.

Death of Henry Winthrop. [*Life and Letters of John Winthrop*, Vol. II., p. 33.]

"They saw," etc. [Family records quoted in the above, p. 35.]

II.

PAGE 130.

" My son Henry," etc. [Same.]

The great house. [Same, p. 49.]

PAGE 131.

The empty cask. [*Boston Newsletter*, Jan. 4, 1733.]

"Almost in every family," etc. [Edward Johnson's *Wonder-Working Providence*, Chap. XVII., p. 38.]

Lady Arbella's death Mather says: "Of those who dyed soon after their first arrival, not the least considerable was the lady *Arabella*, who left an earthly *paradise* in the family of an *Earldom*, to encounter the sorrows of a *wilderness*, for the entertainments of a *pure worship* in the *house of God;* and then immediately left that wilderness for the Heavenly *paradise*, . . . But as for her virtuous husband, Isaac Johnson, Esq.,

> 'He try'd
> To live without her, liked it not, and dy'd.'"

[*Magnalia*, Book I., p. 71.]
  "**Left that wilderness,**" etc. [Same.]
  "**She took,**" etc. [Same.]

Anne Pollard. [*Memorial History*, Vol. I., p. 521.]
Winthrop's house stood on what is now Washington Street, opposite School Street. It was probably at first a plain, rough structure with window-panes of oiled paper. He thought Dudley's house too fine with its "wainscotting and adorning," and told him he "did not well to bestow such cost" upon it. Dudley answered that "it was for the warmth of his house, and the charge was little, being but clapboards nailed to the wall in the form of wainscot." [*Life and Letters*, 94.]
  Winthrop and Dudley fell into a quarrel over their houses and their ways of conducting public affairs, but the quarrel ended in a firmer friendship, and, in 1638, when they were

choosing a thousand acres of land apiece in Concord, they named two stones which marked the boundary between their possessions, the "Two Brothers, in remembrance that they were brothers by their children's marriage and did so brotherly agree." [*Life and Letters*, 93–101.] "The two great stones are standing to this day, and are still known as the Two Brothers." [*Memorial History.*]

"**About two in the morning,**" etc. [Winthrop's *History of New England*, Vol. I., p. 40, under date of Sept. 30, 1630.]

PAGE 137.

The name "Boston" was given to the town on the 17th of September, 1630. The Colony Records say, "It is ordered that Trimountain shall be called Boston."

III.

PAGE 139.

"**On February 5th,**" etc. [Mather's *Magnalia*, Vol. I., Book II., p. 111.]

PAGES 140–143.

The Plymouth Thanksgiving. [See p. 66.]

Chickataubot. Thomas Dudley writes in his letter to the Countess of Lincoln: "Upon the river of Naponset neere to the Mattachusetts fields dwelleth Chicka Talbott, who hath betweene 50 and 60 subjects. This man least favoreth the English of any Sagamore . . . wee are acquainted with, by reason of the old quarrel betweene him and those of Plymouth, wherein hee lost 7 of his best men, yet hee lodged one night the last winter at my house in a friendly manner."

PAGE 144.

"The governor, being at his farmhouse," etc. [*History of New England*, Vol. I., p. 74.]

IV.

PAGES 147-152.

The first church. [Same, p. 104.] The first building stood on what is now State Street. Wilson was appointed " teacher " of the church.

Mr. John Cotton arrived Sept. 4, 1633, in the ship Griffin. He was associated with Mr. Wilson as teacher of the church. [Palfrey, Vol. I., Chap. IX., p. 377.]

"**The governour and some company with him,**" etc. [Winthrop, Vol. I., p. 82.]

"**The governour, Mr. Nowell,**" etc. [Same, p. 83.]

"**In an hard and long winter,**" etc. [Mather, Vol. I., Book II., p. 112.]

Winthrop died March 26, 1649. He is buried in the King's Chapel burying-ground.

"**Yea, the governour,**" etc. [Mather, Vol. I., Book II., p. 112.]

"**The terror of the wicked,**" etc. [Same, p. 109.]

INDEX.